# *Bold*

# *Accountability*

## *A Peter Berk Novel*

## BY STEVEN VARNELL

Disasters are a matter of bad timing; the critical moment when a series of events coincide with catastrophic results.

## Other Non-Fiction books by Steven Varnell

Criminal Interdiction
Tactical Survival
Behavior Analysis and Interviewing Techniques
Statement Analysis for Law Enforcement – An ISS Course Workbook
The Complete Interdiction and Survival Strategies
Eliciting Effective Interviews and Interrogations: An ISS Course Guide
Advanced Interviews and Interrogations Class

# 1

"Do it now!"

He pulls the night vision goggle from the top of his head over his eyes. They are not the play type kids use to see a few feet ahead. This is the ATN NVM 14-4 model with an aim point, flip-up head adapter and weapon mount. Looking through the goggle the night lit up in an eerie green glow as they eased towards the fence. He can see the area like he was approaching at dusk, except in a bright eerie green glow. His passenger insisted on this expensive equipment even though he can find his way with the available light. Jose knows by the way he carries himself that tonight's passenger is of high value and not another Mexican refugee.

The two men in the car crept down the dirt road that shows no signs of recent traffic. Without lights, detection by anyone on either side is doubtful after midnight on Tuesday morning. The "coyotes" or smugglers who study the routines of the United States Customs and Border Patrol selected the time. Across the border the government has spent their reserves chasing illegals over the weekend which are always the busiest time for law enforcement.

The passenger tells the driver in a low harsh voice, "Pay attention to what you are doing! There can be no mistakes. I must get to the exact spot undetected. You hit something, and I will..." He stops catching himself.

Jose speaks Spanish under his breath while driving, "Listen, calm down, everything is alright! I told you I have done these many times. Calmese señor."

He hesitates a moment his mind thinking of what he has said and to whom before adding, "por favor."

Here in the Mexican State of Sonora, the passengers name is Tomas Guerra Vega. Fauzi in other places. He looks and speaks Spanish fluently.

"I said pay attention, not tell me what to do."

Jose keeps driving as Tomas wonders if it is his real name. Jose is the most common name south of the border. Jose's mind races thinking how much this guy makes him nervous.

They approach the fence, stop, get out of the car, and walk to the border. Five strands of barbed wire strung between old poles and new steel spikes separate the two countries. It looks like a scene from a western meet's sci-fi movie. Another unfulfilled half-hearted effort of America to protect its borders. Tomas uses his night vision goggle to look around the area and sees nothing. Jose is nervous just by the way the other man stands. No doubt about it. He's a dangerous man.

He reaches into his pocket and removes a Marlboro cigarette and lit it with his Zippo lighter to help calm his nerves. The kerosene fueled flame wavers in the wind and illuminates his face. To the north, high above on a hill in the American state of Arizona, a lone Border Patrol agent sits and watches. To the southwest, Agent Dale Thomas sees a light for a moment and begins watching for any sign of activity.

# 2

To assure the success of tonight's single car movement, other groups cross at locations both east and west for the last week. These are suicide runs to the coyotes and unsuspecting "pollos" or chickens as the smugglers call their human cargo. They know that once found and arrested, Customs and Border Protection agents will ship the "pollos" back to their country of origin. The smugglers don't care. They get another payday when they return to try again another night. People pay their life savings for this opportunity and are always surprised when their "guide" disappears after crossing the border. For the coyotes, it is a paid cat-and-mouse game. For the "pollos", all that they have is at stake. They are unaware how expendable their lives are, but if they knew, would try to cross anyway.

The traffickers are paid in advance to move people over the border and don't care if the U.S. Border Patrol catch any or all of them. What is important on some nights is the attention they draw so their high value targets can cross elsewhere. These high value targets are drug mules and others who are often non-Mexicans and do not speak Spanish but have lots of money to pay. Their reasons for crossing are different but to the cartel's, it is about money.

These suicide runs over the weekend caused the Border Patrol to transfer agents to cover leaving only a skeleton crew for this stretch of desert border. That is the plan but there is always a risk in illegal crossings. In few other countries are the borders of so many problems separated by so little as here between the United States and Mexico.

Jose has traveled this route so many times he recognizes each bush and cactus and ravine. To anyone else each turn looks like the next. They become lost moving in circles never realizing that with each step they are closer to the trail they already walked. He received triple his standard pay and keeps the equipment. He knows the gear has long-term value and will make him more money as "pollos" seek his services to help them across the border. He can charge them more than the standard smuggler and justify it with a promise of a better chance of success with his "special equipment". Tonight however, he does not feel right and wants this trip to end.

Most of the coyotes are just above poor in Mexico. There is no middle-class south of the border; you are either rich or poor. The rich get richer and the poor stay poor unless they involve themselves in an illegal activity. With these activities come risk. With risk comes reward. The risk is understood, and the reward is greater than most will ever know, and few ever reach. People act out of fear and not respect of the smugglers. Only the guns of the organization are bigger, not the people.

Tomas met Jose in the small town of Fronteras. He needed a reliable and experienced guide to take him close to a specific place on the United States border. Contact with the cartel led to the extra border traffic and the meeting with Jose. Jose knew of his importance and planned the trip north along Highway 17 before turning east on Highway 2 west of Aqua Prieta. From there they stay east of the city in the desert, their destination unknown until they are traveling. Tomas promised to pay him $10,000.00, the most Jose had ever seen at one time for giving someone directions; $5,000.00 up front with the balance due at the crossing. Tomas told him to get him into the United States without problems from the authorities. Nothing more. Over the border and leave.

Tomas chose the day and location with help from cartel scouts for its vastness and escape opportunities and studied the routes with care. With the suicide runs arranged elsewhere and no moon, this stretch of border should be clear tonight. He has planned for this and will see it through at all cost.

Once your eyes adjust to the landscape you can see the larger and darker objects. Why take unnecessary risk and increase the odds of detection? Sound travels forever in this vastness and no one can determine the exact location without sight. People have no idea how dangerous it is this far into the desert. There are no towns, streetlights, or houses, just vast emptiness. There is no way to see across this night and why Jose was guiding and Tomas supplied the night vision.

Jose closed the lighter and the flame left a momentary impression of itself in his vision and he tried to refocus to the dark. Noticing the leftover image of the blue flicker he looked around and closed his eyes as if now was the time to protect his vision. He re-opened them to see if it had faded when he felt something sting with a burning sensation on his neck. It started on his left side and moved to the right. The feeling was odd, not yet painful. He reached up with his right hand and felt a large opening in his throat as panic and shock set in and he dropped the cigarette to the desert floor and grasped the opening with both hands. A thick warm liquid flowed down his arms and chest. Wide-eyed he tried to speak but could not. He stumbled in a circle desperate to understand what was happening yet feeling weaker. His heart was racing only to pump blood faster. Unable to breathe well nor scream, Jose became weak and dizzy as he smelled the metallic odor of his own blood and realized death was approaching yet was powerless to slow it. Dropping to his knees and then to his face, he bled out on the desert floor, blood pooling into a thick paste as the heavy fluid became absorbed by the sand. His body twitching less as life left.

4

Tomas stamped out the orange glowing cigarette into the dirt and eased closer and whispered in his ear, "I told you to be quiet and no lights, pendajo!"

These odors of death will attract scavengers from the desert and Jose will become another sun-bleached skeleton in the highway of death. Tomas, not paying attention to the moment of chaos he created continued to scan the desert for any signs of movement. He has no tolerance for un-disciplined people.

After removing all the items from Jose's pockets including most of the money he had paid, Tomas took the packs he had in the trunk of the car. He sat in the brush watching with his goggles the distant desert for any sign of movement. He cleaned his knife and placed it back into the scabbard on his belt. There is no concern about leaving a body and car in the desert. The Mexican government pays no attention to the bodies found each day because of the drug war throughout the country. It is just another smuggling murder and the authorities know not to investigate. These are the corruptive actions within the police forces across Mexico to aid the cartel's when they need to eliminate a rival due to the lack of money, still the root of most evil. The cartel will not be happy with their loss. They willingly get people to work for them who are protected by association. Extra money will take care of their loss so easily replaced.

CBP Agent Dale Thomas is looking down into Mexico from his elevated position. It is not his normal range of patrol. He has been here several times to help when the area had higher than usual activity. There are three agents on patrol, but two arrested a group earlier and were transporting them back to Douglas, Arizona for processing. Other agents were called into the region after midnight to compensate for the activity. Groups of illegals made runs to the north one at a time and sometimes in coordinated attempts to overwhelm the agents earlier in the evening. Ground sensors or seismic activity devices notice the pressure changes as people walk near them, are placed at various locations, and moved regularly to prevent smugglers from recognizing the sensor area. The idea is they can hit a sensor, signal their position today and tomorrow avoid that area. By changing the sensor locations, the best-case scenario is that the sensors are moved to a place used to avoid its last area and again signal the site of the aliens.

Agent Thomas thought the light down at the border appeared as a small flickering flame and not a flashlight. More "tonks" were on the way. "Tonks" is another of many names used for illegals that cross the border everyday while the politicians do little more than lip service to stop the invasion.

5

# 3

Tomas Guerra Vega is Venezuelan born from the Barrio la Ceiba on the outskirts of Caracas. He never met his father and his mother named him Jesus Monteverde Sanchez, yet few knew him by that name. As with other barrios in the region, Ceiba is its own city built by the poorest of people on the fringes of the capital where most dreamed of opportunity as the economy of Venezuela continued to crash. People numbering in the thousands came to the cities for something better. What they found was an existence worse than what they had fled. What they saw were thousands clamoring in the same areas for the same promise that never arrives. Over time, they built shanty homes on the hillsides. Electricity and water are diverted by theft into these communities that lacks sanitation and dependability. The utility companies will not disconnect any of the services, afraid of reprisals. It is easier to pass the cost to the cities paying population. These shanty communities continue to grow until they consumed areas as large as Caracas itself.

They are lawless where mobs and gang's rule. The police will not enforce the law in these areas without the help of the military. There are no streets and travel is by foot along the many winding paths and stairways built on the side of mountains. Gravity controls the sanitation flowing down through the washouts in the mud of the hills. It is a common joke among the residents that the best water is always above you. Food is grown, stolen, shared and sometimes bought through local homemade stores.

Jesus grew up here and learned to endure. The times were hard and only hard people survived. His mother managed however possible to care for her own. An elder is anyone who reached middle age because they can survive for just so long in Ceiba years. His mother hardened by the environment was going to have a son who was tough. By the time he turned 12, Jesus stayed away more than at home. He proved himself within the barrios of thieves. She cared not because it was hard enough to feed herself much less take care of Jesus. In other countries she appears cruel or unfit as a mother. True in a civilized world, but not in Barrio la Ceiba. Life or death here exist on the simple decisions we take for granted and they see as existence. Famed Psychiatrist Victor Frankel once described survival changes in Nazi concentration camps as, "An abnormal response to an abnormal situation is normal behavior." People of the barrio see themselves and their neighborhood as normal but to the outsider, the barrios is hell.

Conditions in Venezuela began to worsen with the decision to accept Socialism. It is an idea that looks good on paper but has never worked. Socialist need to control and always becomes an authoritarian state. The leader of the state takes everything, pays loyalist, and arms them well. He takes the weapons from the populace that keeps him in power and makes the people weak. Power always exists with money and guns; the guns to control the people and anyone who stands up to his authority and money for personal wealth and more guns. Step hard enough on those who oppose you and weaken their will to resist with thoughts of, "How can we do anything; they have all the guns." It is the same plight in any socialist country if the leadership can survive for a generation; the generation becomes more dependent on the state and will give up its resistance. Cuba is a prime example of this authoritarian socialistic government control. The population used to resist but over decades, the older generations die off and the new ones believe that the State supplies all their needs and lose their will to fight. Another of many reasons why socialism has never worked as a governing process.

Flights arrive in Caracas from oversees that do not accept passengers. These flights carry only members of Iran's Republican Guard and Qods forces to and from Tehran and Caracas. They are Iran's elite fighting forces and considered loyal to their cause and to their Supreme leader. The growth of worldwide expansion in the name of Iran and Allah. The flights travel between Iran, Syria, Lebanon, and Venezuela via Iran Air and Conviasa, the airline of Venezuela. This is part of the socialists' government new arrangement with their friend the President of Iran. According to both less than trustworthy world leaders, the flights are for businesspeople, tourists, and the prospect of vacations between Venezuela and the Islamic Republic of Iran with a fun-filled layover in Syria or Lebanon. There is one thing that these countries do have in common, the terrorist organization Hezbollah.

Hezbollah is the fighting arm of Iran and headquartered in Lebanon. Members of Hezbollah, Qods, and the Guard work to train the Venezuelan army while helping smuggle guns and drugs to finance troops and their cause. They also train The Revolutionary Armed Forces of Columbia – Peoples Army or FARC guerrillas against the democratic government who without American support, would fall. They are another anti-imperialism organization common throughout South America, backed by both communist and Islamic states. This philosophy has been described since the 1950's as dominoes falling one against another. Americans are self-absorbed with social media and drug legalization. Their attention is not overthrown governments leading to more destabilization in South America and a growing terroristic threat to the United States.

Jesus is the right person for specialized training with these groups. Not only is he street smart, he also has nothing to lose. Venezuela and other poor South American countries are the perfect breeding grounds for terrorist organizations. Jesus understands the trivial things that matter most. His Iranian trainers often single him out because of his name. Devout Muslims view the name as the Christian biblical version and not the common Spanish pronunciation. To avoid the problems and show his loyalty to the cause, he changed his name to Fauzi, one of the most common names in Venezuela. No one will ever know him again by any other name.

Fauzi changed his last name to Guerra, meaning war. He would have to change his name again for the upcoming operation in America. This time to Tomas. Fauzi sounded too Muslin and will draw attention if U.S. authorities arrest him. He is 38 years old and a trained operator of Hezbollah. The approach is perfect. A Spanish-born immigrant crossing into the United States will not draw attention. He has expectations of destruction. An organized attack against the evil giant, the United States. Others had crossed the border ahead of him with false identities for years. If caught, they return to Mexico and then cross again. The Border Patrol calls all non-Mexican aliens OTM's or Other Than Mexican's and they attract more attention before returned to their home countries. Return travel from Mexico is a lot easier than return travel from Venezuela.

One other was sent ahead of Fauzi and others will follow for this operation. No one had the complete plans, though Fauzi knew who was where. Each had a Spanish bible and instructions to wait until contacted. The bibles included markings not to attract attention. They were all told if caught they will get to keep the bibles because Americans never take away articles of someone's faith. Fauzi stared at the symbols in his book before leaving with Jose earlier in the day. It is an old forgotten code and appeared on the page as:

"Hieroglyphic markings or simple doodling?" he thought the first time he was shown the code. Maybe his handlers had used an ancient language of Mohammed.

He had hoped it was something similar. Adding the actual words of Allah to the teachings of the infidels is a great insult. He smiled thinking back, but now he had the key to the code. He looked up as Jose approached him in a restaurant to begin the journey towards the border.

"Good morning Señor." Jose said to the man seated.

"Good morning. Tea?" was the prepared response.

"Yes, follow me and we will discuss your intentions."

Leaving Jose's body in the desert Fauzi stepped up to the border fence. He took one last look around and stepped into the United States. He moved with caution and stopped at the first clump of trees. The plan is to move northwest where he will pick up Highway 80 north of Douglas, Arizona. From there he will stay in Rodeo, New Mexico and then up towards Interstate 10. His original plans are to stop and bury his identification. He had a package sent ahead with documentation to convert him to an Arizona resident. He did not plan on killing his guide and leaving the body so close to the crossing. The new plan is to go a mile or more away before burying the documents. He moves northwest and realizes he is traveling too fast and making too much noise and stops to listen a moment.

# 4

Agent Dale Roberts has been with the United States Customs and Border Patrol for 7 years. He was a city patrol officer in St. Louis, Missouri before joining CBP. He spent his first 5 years at the San Diego sector. The government has each region of the border broken into what it calls "sectors". Each sector is named after the primary city and headquarters for that area. The sector covers certain areas regardless of state lines. The El Paso sector in Texas covers the area east of El Paso and all southern New Mexico. The Tucson Arizona sector covers the southern border of the state except for the Yuma and Wellton areas. Roberts works from the Tucson sector, which includes Douglas, Arizona located across from the Mexican city of Aqua Prieta. He has been here for 2 years and tonight he's on foot in the desert region east of Douglas after parking his truck to the north. Agent Roberts is with two other agents when sector calls them after midnight to report a triggered sensor and they moved to the area to intercept.

When a sensor signals movement, they cannot tell how many people are in the area. The dispatch center receives the hit and if it is in a populated area, they activate cameras to see what triggered the signal. At the same time, they radio field agents the information so they can move in to apprehend them. If they arrive late and the people have already traveled past, the agents will move to various "cuts" or dirt roads built north of each other and laid east and west. The Border Patrol ties old tires to the back of their trucks and drag them along cut dirt roads called "draglines". Anyone moving north must cross these draglines and leave their footprints. Based on when the they last drug the trail tells the agents the age of the prints. Driving the cuts shows how far the people have traveled to pinpoint their location. Agents Carlos Sierra and Eddie Gonzalez are with Dale Roberts in the sector tonight.

Agent Gonzalez drives two cuts north of the border looking for fresh footprints called "cutting sign". Once found he can determine the number of people and follow to overtake the group. Agent Sierra takes the first cut and Roberts starts following the tracks. Other agents when available move to help because they know who is where and what they are doing. But not tonight. Sierra and Gonzalez drive along the east-west trails to find the tracks of the same group. If they do, the tracking can begin at that spot and avoid tiring the agents with unnecessary walking distances, except for the following agent who tonight is Roberts.

Finding these groups are important because not only have they broken the laws of the country, but the areas traveled are desolate with no water or help if they're abandoned by their "coyote". Countless numbers of men, women, and children disappear each year in the deserts. In this desolate and moisture stealing heat, a person's body goes through stages. The first sign of trouble is cramps. Before the onset of cramps, you are heat stressed. You try to drink water, but the desert takes it as you sweat. You are not taking in enough fluids to keep up with the loss and the condition worsens. You keep moving and the cramps start. They are not cramps alleviated by stretching. Their entire body hurts and is caused by the loss of electrolytes such as salt, potassium, and calcium. Physical exhaustion and dizziness begin. The victim will continue a downward spiral unless conditions improve.

Next, exhaustion caused by an excessive loss of body fluids takes over. This is characterized by profuse sweating, cool, clammy, pale skin, and a weak, rapid pulse. Victims become lightheaded, experience chills or shivering and are unable to concentrate. If left untreated, this can progress to the final stage; heat stroke. Heat stroke causes mental confusion and/or unconsciousness and shock. The person will not sweat, and their skin will be hot, dry, and red. Their pulse is rapid and their breathing fast and deep. At this stage, they have less than an hour to start reversing their core temperature or die.

The terrain is devoid of color except tan and some green brush. It is a dangerous place even without the border politics with scorching dry heat in the day and cold freezing temperatures at night. Every plant or animal will bite, stick, or sting. Spend any time in the desert plains and you become mesmerized by its vastness and beauty. Everywhere you look there are changes from dry arroyos to flat mesas, and out to the plains. Wonder too far for too long and you will disappear. Water is more valuable than gold and needed or else you will dry up, die, and wither into the landscape. Unlike the images we see of the Sahara, the southwest is deceiving and alive. There are Mesquite trees, creosote bushes, sagebrush, and cacti of many types. Travel off track a little and one can wonder to nowhere. It is wise to know where you are and ready for any outcomes in these deserts and thus the popularity of the "coyotes".

Agent Carlos Sierra is driving west at the first cut to the north of the signal when he spots the marks. He leans out the window using his spotlight and see's the sharp outlines of the shoe edges and knows they are fresh.

"Hey Dale, Eddie. I've got em. Looks like about a dozen. They walked across the cut heading north. Start moving my way at angles and we will meet."

"Roger that." Both Dale and Agent Eddie Gonzalez responded.

Agent Sierra parks and is following the prints. Roberts is walking north coming up behind him. Gonzalez has not seen any prints and knows they are all moving towards him. He parks his truck and moves south and waits.

"Hey Dale, Eddie is north of me have you reached the cut yet?"

"Yeah, I got it, but I am at the start trail. Ya'll stay on them and I'll follow for any runners."

"Roger that."

Often when the coyotes believe the agents are following, they will break from the group and reverse back to the border and the safety of Mexico. When this happens, members of the group panic, separate, and try to find their way back south. These breakouts are called "runners". Agent Dale Roberts made his way to a hilltop and watched with his night vision goggles for any other movement in the desert.

Agent Sierra starts gaining on the group and as expected, their guide abandons them. They heard the trucks as they were cutting sign both ahead and behind them and they all sat down to hide and prevent noise. As Sierra moved closer the aliens run to spread out and lay down in the brush.

"I see them!" Sierra says over the radio with excitement.

"To my right, a little under the brush. No Te Muevas!"

Gonzalez, who is ahead of the group, begins to move south and help grab them as they run or shelter in place. Together they arrest seven members of the group and an unknown number escape.

"I don't know how many is in the group, but it was more than this." Sierra said.

To the south, Dale listened to the arrest and radios the others.

"You guys alright?"

"Yeah we're good." Gonzalez responds.

"Okay. I'm gonna settle in for a while and watch. Let me know when you get back in the area."

"Roger that."

He is in a good place to spot any north or southbound traffic. At 3:45 AM, Roberts is watching from a high bluff when he sees a small light to the southeast. He radios Eddie Gonzalez.

"Eddie can you hear me?"

"Go ahead Dale; I'm heading back about 30 out."

"I have a light, small and fast. It could be runners from the earlier group or a new one."

"Alright, anyone else out there with you?"

"No, haven't heard anybody on the radio in a while."

"Stay put and I will be there in a minute."

"Ok, I'm moving closer to see what we have."

Dale moves out to the south to position himself to intercept the aliens if they travel northwest towards the town and roads of Douglas.

# 5

Hezbollah recruited Fauzi as a para-military member and trained him in the jungles south of Caracas. The Iranians and Hezbollah trainers set up the camps to condition and teach recruits their art of war. They watch for those who stand out in ways considered useful in guerrilla tactics against Israel and the United States. The non-Muslim world is a target, but the "Big and Little Satan's" always come first if the opportunities present themselves.

Hezbollah is a Shiite terrorist faction created and funded by both Iran and Syria, armed and equipped with Soviet weapons. Trained in modern warfare tactics, they use satellite communications, advanced anti-tank weapons, and Semtex plastic explosives. They prey on the poor and disadvantaged to fulfill suicide missions without the loss of trained soldiers in psychological or psy-ops warfare. One well-placed suicide attack can create long-term terror for the residents.

In their early years, Hezbollah specialized in kidnappings and suicide attacks. Who can forget the suicide attack that killed American Marines in Beirut? This single act was responsible for withdrawing U.S. forces from Lebanon. They have always worked in small units with autonomous functions to carry out missions on their own. Their leaders never wear uniforms identifying them as commanders. Their soldiers always work and operate within general populations for concealment. As Shiite Muslims, they are opposites of Sunni Muslims. They each share the Muslim teachings but differ in their view of who will lead the Muslim faith.

It all began after the death of the Prophet Muhammad and who was to take over the leadership of the Muslim nation. Sunni Muslims agreed to elect their leader from among those capable of the job. The word "Sunni" in Arabic means "one who follows the traditions of the Prophet." Sunni's make up 85% of the faith including the founders of al Qaeda.

Shia Muslims believe leadership should stay within the Prophet's own family. They should be from among those appointed by him or among Imams appointed by God Himself. The word "Shia" in Arabic means "a supportive party of people."

Because one group believes the most qualified should lead and the other believes direct descendants or "Imams" or holy men should lead, thus began the eternal strife of the faith that has lasted for centuries.

Handpicked for the assignment, Fauzi and six other recruits trained hard and absorbed the information like a sponge. The training is serious and dangerous as only the best will survive. One died during the training and two other recruits sent back to be with the regular forces never arrived. They failed to meet the physical and mental needs of self-sacrifice. The families of the deceased are told their sons and daughters have died in service to the country and encouraged to convince other families to donate their children.

Recruits are "infidels" or one without faith by their Muslim trainers. They have not earned the trust and may never because of Muslim intolerance of any other faith. The recruits know the brutality of their Muslim allies, still often better than life in the barrios.

Fauzi and the others learned survival techniques and the use of weapons, explosives, surveillance, and anti-surveillance tactics. They train in self-defense, knife tactics, unarmed combat, to use available items as weapons, and how to set and avoid booby-traps. They trained as Hezbollah Special Forces in theory, but, known only to their trainers, they were expendable cannon fodder. They were schooled on Islam and the teachings of the Prophet. The training de-sensitized them to death including that of innocent civilians, which is acceptable when it helps achieve an end to their mission. This part came natural to the recruits.

"Captain Mubarraqa, assalamu alaikum (how are you)," said Sergeant Nasrallah of the Hezbollah training forces.

"Assalamu alaikum, Sergeant. How are our new soldiers?"

"I believe they are learning and progressing well, in sha' Allah (if Allah wills)."

Sgt. Nasrallah says, "It is of one of the teams that I want to talk to you about."

"Alright, then talk, I have some time."

"It is my belief that they are the team you asked me to watch for Captain."

"After 7 teams passing through here, I was beginning to wonder if they would ever develop or maybe it was whoever was selecting."

Sergeant Nasrallah had taken the words as an idle threat because he alone had handpicked the candidates.

"I am sorry Captain, but when you first spoke to me about the special team, I knew there would be issues in developing them. I never thought they would be so hard to train. They have the bodies; they do not always have the mind. They come from poor backgrounds and no education. Most qualify as martyrs, but to train them to reason on their own is hard. None of them are true Muslim and so without the full support of Allah."

"Sergeant, Allah will help whoever comes to his worship and leaves his old life behind. We all know la ilaha illallah (there is no lord worthy of worship except Allah). Body and soul will convert in sha' Allah (If Allah wills)."

13

"This is why I asked you here today," says Sgt. Nasarallah with a grin. "I have tried to train individuals within a distinct group to work together as a team. I thought if they came together and trained, the brotherhood would begin to instill teamwork. Unfortunately, I was wrong and learned that these recruits were mentally unprepared to trust in one another. They have stolen, injured, raped, and killed for so long, in their minds, survival is a solo act."

Captain Mubarraqa nodded his head as he turned from the window and looked at his Sergeant and said, "So with this mentality what is it that you decided to do?"

Again, Sgt. Nasarallah grinned and said, "We were forced to lose more than usual, but I brought together six of the best recruits. Accustomed to self-survival and not teamwork, it was difficult in the beginning. Out of that group, one was lost through carelessness and we sent two others home. I think I have three that have formed a team."

"So how did you instill this teamwork, Sergeant?"

"I allowed the others to take the two who failed home." He said with a smile before continuing. "They learned in a language they understood what happens to failure. This action shows their will to follow all orders or face the same consequence."

"Good Sergeant. That is why I chose you to oversee the training. I like what you have done and will send information to the other camps the success of your methods to help them understand dedication to our missions. Show me who you have chosen, and I will explain the next stage of the training."

Sergeant Nasarallah was pleased with himself and the words of the captain as he said, "ma sha' Allah!" (Whatever Allah wants)

His emotions kept deep inside for an air of humility in the face of his commanding officer.

# 6

Agent Dale Roberts moved in the dark and rough terrain without running from the bluff where he first saw the flicker of light in the distance. The night is dark with no moon. He uses night vision goggles to navigate the various trails and around the bush and rocks. His pace slows as he nears the location to set up an ambush. He knows the place where his odds are best to intercept anyone traveling north. He positions himself near two common paths that come close to one another. One was an actual beaten down game and traveler trail. The other was an arroyo. Arroyo is a Spanish word translated as a brook and is a dry river or creek bed that gets deeper each time the heavy seasonal rains arrive. The ground is so dry and hard from the heat and under layered with rock, rain never soaks down. It moves and collects into these deep beds drowning any creature in its way. As these torrential rains fall and gather in the arroyos, the water runs downhill into the valleys. Sediment carries with the water and there is a collection of the sand left over from the dry heat of the desert where the stream ends.

Dale sat against the west wall of the arroyo to rest his legs with his back reclined and listened. His own panting breaths fill his ears along with his pounding heart. He uses autonomic breathing techniques to slow his heart rate and takes a deep breath through his nose, expels it through his mouth, and repeats the process several more times until his system approaches a normal rate. This is the only way to lower the heart rate to regain control of the other senses. He waits knowing he is ahead of whoever is there, if they come this way.

He removes his goggles to keep his night vision. The bright green view will take a minute to overcome. So dark is this night that his primary sensory channel is useless without the goggles, so he listens for the sounds of movement. He pays attention as the night wind blows through the creosote and across the shifting sand. There is little to disturb the breeze and the desert fills with noise.

"If anyone approaches, I'll hear them." He says to himself placing the radio earpiece in his left ear to prevent the sound of any radio chatter escaping and still hear the night sounds through his right ear.

Sound carries long distances in the desert when still and further with the wind. The wind will carry sounds like water carries the sand in an arroyo. He checks the wind and it is out of the south and in his favor. The breeze will carry all sounds and smells to him from anyone who moves below. The trap is set and all he can do is wait.

Tomas was moving to the northwest towards Douglas. Even though he had memorized the area from a map, it is not the same when traveling on foot. Worse in the dark. The map shows elevations but not the bush and debris. A rental car is waiting for him in another's name at the Douglas International Airport. He knew this was one of the most dangerous moments of the mission. Since September 11, 2001, the United States has created agencies that have become bloated and ineffective. They could shut down the borders if they wanted to, but the American population is divided and weak. They care more for illegal immigrants and their lack of rights than the rights of their own citizens. Tomas often spoke of how America was ripe for an assault. Their people want instant gratifications, not have to tolerate the long tolls of war.

In planning for the day, Tomas knew that E. Geronimo Trail Road was over 2 kilometers north of the border. It is an east-west corridor that leads to the airport and heavily patrolled. It would be a good landmark to follow to his destination. He carried GPS equipment, but decided against its use. Imagine the investigations that would take place with the capture of a Mexican illegal with sophisticated electronics. He learned English as part of his training so he can communicate with others or pretend he does not understand if captured. He was taught how to gather intelligence by playing dumb and listening. He remembers what his trainers always said, "You have two ears and one mouth. Listen twice as much as you talk."

Tomas continued through the desert. Stopping on occasion to watch and listen; nothing. He is pleased with the decision to earlier send groups of unsuspecting aliens through the area. The idea was his and the sounds of the desert told him of its success. He began to move again with caution and yet, more confidence.

Dale Roberts remained quiet and calm. From the darkness of the trail, he heard a sound he recognized from many times before; footsteps. Whoever was approaching is stepping slow and calculated. He heard the sand crush and spread under the walkers' shoes and on a few twigs that crackled under foot.

He radioed. "Eddie, you read me?"

"Go ahead Dale. I am approaching the area at the bluff."

"Ok, park up there near my truck and move southwest to the arroyo and trail junction."

"What do you have?"

"Footsteps. Gotta go." Dale replied in a whispered tone.

"Don't do anything till I get closer."

There was no reply.

"Hold on, I'll be down there in a few."

He had been in the same scenario in the past. Sounds in the dark, a whispered call out on the radio, you hear others respond but it interferes with the surrounding sounds. Pull out the earpiece to focus on the surprise and in a few moments, it will not matter. Gonzalez parked his truck and moved in the dark towards the location.

# 7

In Miami, Florida, Peter Berk is waking in the Four Seasons Hotel on Brickell Avenue. It has been a tiresome day and the intensity carried over to the night. He lives local but was asked to oversee a meeting and conference at the hotel all the while continuing his regular investigations. Sleep had become a luxury and a full night sleep was an event of his childhood. As with most people who work, see, and experience difficult events repeatedly over time, sleep interruptions are common. They learn to sleep light. He is ready for a cup of coffee but is not about to make it here, even in this hotel. Berk like all cops knows all the things that happen to in-room coffee pots. Room service never cleans them. Kids think it's funny to pee in the pot and cycle the brew. In a worst-case scenario, people cook methamphetamine in these small pots. A better scenario is to watch for the single brew pots that use pods and disposable cups to catch the coffee.

"Nope." he thought to himself. "I'll wait and get coffee downstairs in the lobby."

Dressed in a t-shirt, shorts and Asics shoes, he went downstairs for a workout before most people think about waking. To help warm up, he left his room and tried to close the door quietly, but the automatic locking is loud and reminds him of a prison door. The elevator is in the middle of the hallway so walking to the end he uses the stairway emergency exit. Reaching the ground floor, he has accelerated his heart rate and goes straight to the coffee dispenser in the lobby. Coffee always gives him that jolt he needs to start the day.

Peter Berk was a US Army Special Forces Green Beret before invited to move up to 1st Special Forces Operational Detachment-Delta (1st SFOD-D) or Delta Force. Delta is to the army what the SEALS are to the Navy. The cream of the crop, the best trained best-equipped and most dangerous people on earth. The other operators themselves make their choice of candidates because they get to choose who will stand beside them when the chips are down. He served for 8 years, 6 in the SOF groups, before deciding to move on with his next career path. As with all special operations personnel, he trained continuously. For every month deployed, SOF members train for

3 months. The military, unlike law enforcement, understands it's needs. You can never train enough, which is why they are so good at what they do. Little can occur that surprises them and if it does, those who follow will prepare for whatever occurred to prevent future surprises. The teams activate often, pack up, stand down, pack up, and stand down. Sometimes they packed up and moved to an airfield while other times they trained with mock scenarios and buildings in preparation for work. There are many events in the world and they never know where they might end up each day. Activities against the United States by radical Muslim countries is on the rise, but as most operators learn, you spend all your time preparing for action and see it on occasion. It is good to know they are there when needed. Many groups deploy around the world and Americans never know. The old saying is true; "Sleep well tonight because someone somewhere is standing the wall for you."

After a 30-minute run, Peter heads into the gym and lifts weights. When finished he walked back upstairs to his room to shower, drink coffee he had brought from the lobby, read the newspaper, and watch the news. It is a routine followed to help keep him sharp. After finishing the military, Peter began a career in law enforcement as a State Trooper. He enjoyed the rigors and demand of the job but wanted something different. After 4 years he was accepted into the United States Marshall Service where he was on a fugitive apprehension squad first in New Orleans, Louisiana and now in Miami, Florida. It often reminded him of his work in the teams' the way they track human targets or to blend and ingratiate with the locals to change their hearts and minds. He was well suited for the job but still longed for more.

Dressed and having lunch at the Omni International Mall on Biscayne Boulevard, a man in an Armani suit approached him and stood at his table.

"Can I help you?" Peter said in his best sarcastic voice.

"Yes, you can, but I think I can help you even more."

"Really. How is that?"

"Mr. Berk, I work for a... ."

Peter cut him off while standing and said, "Who the fuck are you and how do you know my name. This had better be good because if you know my name then you sure as hell know what I do and at this moment I am about to put your ass against the wall."

"Hold it a second, my name is Rafael Gomez and I work for an important group. We work for the same people in different roles."

"Let me see some ID."

"We don't carry any official ID and I knew you would be here as part of Operation Mustang."

"Who has that information and does not carry ID? You must be a spook."

"Can we sit down? I would like to talk to you. If you do not like what I have to say, then I will get up and walk out. We never met or talked, and you can go back to jumping court no shows."

Peter stood there a moment and realized he is experiencing those exact described feelings. He enjoyed his job, but it was mundane at times.

Peter says, "Ok, let's sit. I can hear you out."

18

"I work for a group known as the Special Activities Group."

"Yeah, I knew it, CIA. I know about you guys. I was at Eglin Air Force base."

"Yes. You were with the 7SFGA out of Bragg and then at Eglin. You were doing some of your jungle training there as part of your readiness for any Latin American Operations that may arrive. Look Peter, with the Special Operations Group, we operate for the government except in a deniable covert manner."

Peter interrupts, "Plausible deniability."

"Correct. Since 9/11, things have changed. We have always known the world is plotting against the United States. Arab countries that claim to be our allies never are. In their world, it is all right to tell us anything that they choose because we are not a Muslim society and therefore not subject to their interpretation of the Quran. The president has entrusted a lot of responsibility at great personal risk. If you would like to talk some more, call me at this number and we can meet. I have given you my actual name, so you can run all the follow up that you like. When done, get in touch."

Rafael pushes his chair back and starts to stand. Peter stops him and says, "Why should I call you and furthermore why are you telling me this?"

Rafael looked at him, smiled, and said, "For a job."

# 8

Agent Roberts lowers his night vision goggle to his face and watched the trail where he heard the noise. Then he saw him; a single man carrying a backpack. He looks further down the trail and sees no one else. He thinks to himself that he must be a straggler from the earlier groups we found. As the man closes, he prepares to grab him.

Tomas is walking towards E Geronimo trail on his way to the airport. To his left he hears a noise. Agent Roberts came out of the arroyo and yells "Border Patrol! Aquestese, aquestese (down, down)."

Tomas is surprised by how easily he was overtaken and drops to his knees and yells "Agua, agua por favor." He is pretending to be a poor, lost, and thirsty alien. The act allows Tomas to see how many agents are present. His actions put Agent Roberts at ease as he moves in close to arrest the man. He has seen the same scenario played out night after night a hundred times.

Agent Eddie Rodriguez arrives at the bluff and is moving into the area where Dale had told him he would be. In the distance and with the night air moving towards him, he hears what sounds like Dale's voice yell out to get down. He continues and radios Dale his location because he was coming into the area and asking how many are there. Agent Roberts bends over, reaches for his radio, and turns his head to talk in the microphone. He never sees the knife. Tomas slashes across the throat of the agent. He stands and moves behind the bleeding man and drives the knife into his right kidney below the bullet resistant vest. This is an assassin move as the pain is so excruciating, the victim is speechless. After a few seconds, Tomas removes the knife and drives the blade down deep between the neck and collar bone and angles the blade back and forth. Severing the subclavian artery, Agent Roberts dies as he falls to the ground. Tomas hears the other agent on the radio and knows he is close. There is no time to run and cover his tracks so he moves behind some brush to wait and see how many more arrive.

He knew when the other agents arrived, they would shock at the sight of their fellow agent and try to help him. This would cause a delay as they will try to render aid first instead of clearing the area or radioing for help, a common error for officers. Professionals train to clear and secure the area before attempting first aid. Men like

Tomas knew that the one thing worse than one-man down was two or more. He was running the scenario through his mind how he predicts it will play out so he can activate a plan. He adjusts his night goggles on his face. He removes a PB/6P9 silenced Soviet pistol from the pack and waits. He carries the pistol because it was the preferred weapon of Soviet KGB but has since spread across the continents and is popular in Central and Latin America. Not knowing how many agents would arrive, he selected the pistol over the knife. He could not risk anymore problems and planned to kill anyone else. If too many arrived, he could shoot one or two and cause them to have to care for their downed officers and give him time to escape. Otherwise, they will see where he ran and start the chase. He heard the sound coming from the north and up the trail. They were jogging and not trying to cover any noise.

"Dale, can you hear me? Answer your radio."

Eddie was beginning to yell. He walks through the arroyo when he sees a body and stops. Then he sees the uniform and with a shocked burst of energy he yells, "Dale! Are you alright?"

As Tomas predicted, Agent Gonzalez ran over to Agent Roberts lifeless body to try to give first aid. As he drops to his knees, he grabs him and yells, "Dale! What happened?"

Seeing the extent of the injuries he hesitates for a shocked second. He starts to reach for his radio but never made the connection. Something struck him in the forehead. He never heard the sound of the gun go off or if he did, he never reacted to it. The bullet hit him in the forehead above the right eyebrow. The sub-sonic round entered but did not exit. He is dead after falling back from the impact. Tomas picks up the casing and began brushing up his tracks. He must move fast. Knowing he is halfway there, by moving faster he can escape the first perimeter search pattern set up by the police. He plans to be long gone by that time. He knows a few hours will pass before anyone checks on the downed agents and longer before they find them and longer still to bring in the required resources to conduct the search. Tomas must determine if he should move north toward Douglas or take a calculated risk to move south toward Mexico. Thinking about his options he decides to take the risk. Time is on his side and he moves to the south, back towards the border. He is taking heavy steps and maintaining a longer gait. His new steps will appear different and spaced wider as someone running from the scene. They will trace the tracks and move assets to the border. He runs about a quarter of a mile, stops at the edge of hard ground and put socks over his shoes. He turns west and slows his pace. He knows they will track him towards the border. By moving over the harder ground at a slower pace and covering the sharp edges of his shoes, the prints will be less obvious and disappear in the wind faster. By the time they determine that he turned, he will be gone.

# 9

Intrigued by the meeting, Peter placed some calls and completed a few checks. Rafael Gomez is the real deal. Peter places a call to Rafael and says they can meet. Rafael gives him an address and said be there at 11:00 AM.

"By the way." Peter asked. "What kind of interview is it? Should I dress or what?"

"Yes, please wear clothes." Rafael replied and hung up the phone laughing to himself.

Peter is downtown and sees that he has an hour to get ready, so he went ahead and drove to the address. It is a simple building inside a warehouse complex near LeJeune Road and Miami International Airport. Plain building with no signs that has two service bay doors and the standard metal door entrance with a short flight of stairs with handrails on each side. The only thing that looks different are the three cameras. One is over the main door and two others watching the service bay doors. Peter looks behind and sees a fourth camera on the adjacent building, watching the entire face of the address and a view of the parking lot.

Peter approaches the door; a buzzer sounds and he opens it. He steps in and sees a second metal door with a camera. The first door locks behind him. If anyone were to break into the front door, they would find themselves trapped in the small hallway with metal doors on each end and no windows. It reminds him of the entrance to a correctional facility. The second door buzzes, and he opens it and walks into the central office and is greeted by Rafael Gomez.

"Peter, we are glad you came down to see us."

"Thanks."

"Come on back. There are a few others here for the interview."

They walk to the rear of the office space and enter another room. Peter notices as he follows that there are desks, computers, side doors, and a couple of people who look up at him and then back as he passes. They enter the room where he sees two men and a woman. The woman is in her mid-forties and everyone casually dressed in khaki pants and a polo shirt. One of the men is younger in his late 20's, the other in his early 50's. They each stand and introduce themselves, the oldest first.

"Hey Peter. My name is Hatfield, John Hatfield." They shake hands, as he turns towards the other male.

"Peter how are you. I am Jesse Papadopoulas, but most people call me Papadop, Papa, or just plain Dop."

"Glad to meet you." Peter said as he turns towards the woman.

"Peter, this is Sarah Jenkins." They shake hands as Sarah directs him to a chair.

"Please. Have a seat, Peter. Can we offer you something to drink?"

"No thanks, I'm fine."

Sarah stares into an open folder on the desk in front of her before saying, "Well Peter, thanks for coming down. To be straightforward with you we do not have much time. We will need an answer when finished today. This is not a regular job and our work is too important. There is no Human Resources and being here now is taking us away from other work."

"Ok, explain it to me and I will tell you."

"Good." Sarah responds and then continues. "Rafael told you a little about things already. Before we start, I have several documents I need you to review, date, and sign. They are to protect us from information leakage from you.

Peter looks over the paperwork as Sarah continues.

"Anything you see, hear, remember or think you remember, including the location, building and room descriptions, or personnel is classified and you will be prosecuted and sequestered from the outside world for as long as we feel is necessary should you reveal any of our or this information. This includes if you take or refuse the position, forever. Do you understand?"

"Yes." He replied as he signs everything.

"Great. Thank you. The Special Activities Division of the CIA will often bring into its ranks ex-military Special Forces types for the kind of work we do. Even with this background, we will occasionally send you for specialized training when there is time and a specific purpose. Think of it as teaching you how to do it our way."

Peter nodded understanding as she continues.

"The role of the Special Operations Division is sabotage, kidnapping, hostage rescue, and counter terrorism to mention a few. There are other duties like bomb assessments, but we will bring in the ATF or FBI to do those things. The SOD is divided into the ground, maritime, and air branches. Since September 11, there have been some rapid changes to our roles. The government has always left the home territories for the FBI to investigate. The CIA works to protect our foreign interest. This has worked to some degree and alone they have been successful in the dismantling of some obvious organizations. Others have been portrayed as being dismantled by the FBI, but the truth is that they cannot work with the civil obstructions and always be successful."

Peter continued to listen as he nods understanding.

"Many of their cases have been brought to them by us. Not the CIA you think about, but by us. The CIA is still the bureaucratic organization it always has been, and the FBI is still living in the past with their institutions. Despite what you have heard, no one is sharing because they get a budget boost with a successful investigation. It is a game of self-preservation. So, a new group development always works on the outside. Few except at the highest levels know of our existence. Agency budgets are so large, we can siphon a little and they are none the wiser. Various groups for odd jobs use all those extra expenses charged here and there, like a $200.00 toilet seat, ours included. We work both domestic and foreign and conduct any investigation considered as an immediate threat to our country. We receive these threats from all the intel groups as they report their findings up the chain of command. Those operations considered critical go to us and not one of the bureaucracies. We answer to the top and at times pass the intel to the agency that can best place the finishing touches to it. Therefore, it always looks like the various agencies are hard at work protecting the country. It works well by leaving us out because we are never expected. We do not play by the same rules and our restrictions, well, there aren't any. Any questions so far?"

"None."

Peter is sitting there amazed at what he is hearing because the same idea has passed through his mind a thousand times. He often wonders how certain people at certain agencies were ever able to tie their shoes yet solve some of the cases they had.

"Good." said Jesse. "We chose you based on a recommendation from retired Colonel Walter Davis."

Peter is surprised. Colonel Davis was his group commander at Ft. Bragg. After leaving SOF, he oversaw an intelligence division of the Army. It was all adding up.

"We pulled records and training and know you were ODA composition." (Special Forces Operational Detachment – A, or an A-team) As you know as a member of the Green Berets, you were tasked with six primary missions: unconventional warfare, foreign internal defense, reconnaissance, hostage rescue, counter terrorism and of course direct action. Your skill sets merge well with our activities."

"Okay." Peter said.

John Hatfield spoke up for the first time and cut him off. "After that you spent a few years with DELTA with an impressive record. Colonel Davis selected you and gave us your complete service jacket."

Peter was surprised. He had only met Colonel Davis once.

"We are not running on that information only. We see that after completing your military time, you became a State Trooper and then with the U.S. Marshalls. You continued with your dedication to add to your skill sets. Many from your background retire on their past and accomplish little more. We are always looking for that self-leadership and drive."

"Well, that fills in a little of the 'why me' question."

"Ok, Peter." Sarah said, "What do you think? You in or out?"

"Sounds good so far, but I still don't know what you want me to do?"

They all stood up from the table as Sarah said, "Help protect Americans, Peter; Domestic and Foreign, no matter the circumstances. You in or out?"

"In."

"Welcome to the war. Welcome to the "Team". We will give you a week to start if you need time to tie up loose ends."

"I have no loose ends. I can be here tomorrow."

Rafael walked into the meeting and said, "Day after tomorrow Peter, I will meet you here at 0600."

Driving away, Peter's head is spinning with a million questions he is now thinking about to ask and another million things he needs to do.

Thinking aloud he said, "I need to go in and meet with the bosses and give them my resignation."

# 10

Monday morning when Border Patrol Agents Roberts and Gonzalez did not check in, an extensive search began. Ground units searched the area they were patrolling, and a helicopter joined them. Seeing moving people with contrasting colors is hard. Seeing their bodies, dressed in green uniforms and near the walls of the arroyo topped with trees is impossible from the air. They discovered their trucks next to each other as the sun was rising on a high bluff overlooking the area. The search continued until one of the ground units found the bodies. They trailed the footprints from the trucks down to the arroyo and on to the area of a used trail. Both agents found as they died, Agent Gonzalez next to Agent Roberts.

 The agents who knew them reacted in different ways. There is the initial shock as they approach their bodies, but their police-oriented minds prevent them from touch. Others could not approach and cried from a distance. There were those who were angry and cursed out loud. Their thoughts are with the slain officers and their families and how this senseless act affects them forever. They cordon off the area to prevent the destruction of any evidence including footprints. One of the agents, Jaime Cardona, is part Chiricahua Indian. He is the best human tracker in the region. He makes a wide walk around the edges of the scene. He discovers tracks of many people along the trail moving north and of all distinct types of shoes.

 Jaime found only one set of prints that traveled south. These same prints found on the edge showed that after he killed the first agent, he waited for others. He did not find them right away because the person brushed parts of the trail. It is an old trick used by smugglers to remove their prints with bushy limbs from the surrounding area as they walked to conceal themselves. If they discover the brushed area too soon, the marks are obvious. Given time with the wind blowing the area appears the same as the surrounding sand.

 These southbound prints started at the scene and were a different type of shoe. He discovered them northbound along the route before the encounter with the agents. To ensure he was able to find the tracks again Jaime broke off a brush limb. He laid it between the tracks to measure the distance. He verified the distance between other track sets of the same shoe sole. We use the same gait stride between footsteps when walking. If you lose the track, keep measuring with the stick and you will find the next print. These prints showed the person walking slowly in and appearing to run out. Something wasn't quite right about the southbound prints. They may show an exaggerated gate and not running. They appear too far apart and then disappear on a rocky area. He looks further down the trail towards the border as it is the most logical direction and never finds the prints again.

Besides staying to ambush the second agent, another issue that bothered Jaime about this print was the sole belonged to a desert style combat boot. He marked the area and returned to the crime scene to report the information. Whoever had done this appeared to have come out of Mexico and may have returned, but is probably returning to the U.S. side if they ever left at all.

# 11

Peter Berk went to the Marshalls Office the next day to sign his resignation papers and return their equipment. Frank Spoto, the RAC (Resident Agent in Charge) of the Miami Office is at his desk when Peter walks in.

"Now? Have you lost your mind? Are you drunk? Do you need some vacation time to unwind? What the hell is happening here Pete? You never told us anything? I thought everything was alright?"

Peter laughing said, "Frank, would you stop. No one has done anything, I have not been drinking, and I do not need a vacation. I have a better offer."

"You have a better offer? From who?"

"Not another agency, it's in the private sector." Peter said knowing it was not a complete lie. He likes Frank and did not want to cause any problems, but he also knows he cannot tell him about the offer.

Peter said, "I'm thinking of going back to the west coast doing work for a large law firm. The money they offered is too much to pass on."

"I have to tell you that I am shocked. I never saw this coming. You do an excellent job here and I never saw anything different."

"Honest Frank. It has nothing to do with anyone but me. I was not looking to go anywhere else, but a friend called me yesterday and made me an offer. It was too good and I have a plane to catch. If anything comes in for me, you can send it to my apartment. I have to go. Thanks for all you did."

Peter left and drove to the new warehouse office to start work for the no name agency attached to the CIA.

He arrives at the airport warehouse complex before noon. Approaching the door, it buzzed, and he opens it. That door closes and another unlocks giving him access to the room. John Hatfield walks up to the front to greet him.

"Hey Peter, welcome aboard. You're early and that's alright with us. Need help with anything?"

"Thanks. I have a few questions like door access and schedules."

"Follow me. You are starting with a new development. There is no door key access. It is by video surveillance and visual access only. Park wherever you want. You won't be here often anyway. What's a schedule?" Laughing a little. "You'll find little down time. Sarah and Rafael are waiting for you."

Peter thinks to himself, "I like the way things are here already."

They walk into a back room where Sarah and Rafael are talking. The number of television and computer screens surprised him. There are phones all around and a smaller than normal conference table. There are no windows and cork foaming covering the walls and ceilings to help silence the room.

Sarah spoke first. "Good morning, Peter. Is that the name you like to go by? Any nicknames? Are you ready to get to work?"

"Yes mam. Some people call me Pete, but no preferences. Where do we start?"

"First of all, there is no rank among us. We each bring a special skill set to the table and when the information leans to your skill, we listen. Often intel from all of the agencies moves up the chain and if important, will divert to us. We also monitor all the news networks because they are the first to break information around the world."

Rafael laughing said, "Sometimes they report on an event before the event. I wonder who they work for?"

Sarah continues with a quick smile. "There is little paperwork to generate because we do not exist. I will keep contact with those who need contacting and you stay in contact with John, Rafael, or me. If we are not around when you try to get in touch and it's an emergency, talk to one of the others. Otherwise, we will get back to you when we can. You will get what you need to do the job."

She hesitated a moment and said, "Have you been keeping up with the news out of Arizona?"

"No, I haven't stopped long enough to watch the news."

Rafael said, "Yesterday morning, two Border Patrol agents were killed in the desert outside of Douglas. People are calling it drug cartel violence spilling over onto our side. We have a source who said one agent's throat was cut, stabbed in the kidney and in the upper chest and the other shot in the head."

Peter interrupted, "Those are classic assassin techniques."

Rafael continued, "Agents searching found their bodies next to each other. We believe the agent with his throat cut was killed first and the assailant ambushed the other as he came to help his partner. According to tracks, he stayed after killing the first agent to ambush the second. There were tracks leading south away from the scene. The subject was wearing desert style combat boots."

Peter noticed the words used and asked, "Assailant?"

"We know it was one. The drug cartel story could fit. Our Special Forces trained the Zeta's years ago in Mexico. They stopped protecting cartel members and have become a cartel themselves. They are brutal and vicious and trained in the use of military equipment and dress in combat gear. We also know they operate in this area."

Sarah smiled and said, "Peter, even though that is all true and is why there was a day delay in us getting the information, there is another problem."

29

Peter did not say anything. He watched as Sarah looks up at him and says, "The assassin killed the first agent, stayed to ambush the second, made his way towards Mexico, and then cut back northwest, towards Douglas."

"I agree." Peter said. "Why would he not flee back to the safety of Mexico after killing the first agent? To stay and ambush is risky. How would he know that only one other agent would show up?"

"Maybe he didn't care." Rafael responded.

"Agreed. He is on a mission. One that he will see play out regardless." Peter concluded.

# 12

Tomas made it into Douglas and found his car in the airport parking lot as planned with his new identification under the rear seat. He stashed his backpack into the trunk, drove out, and stopped at an all-night Denny's restaurant. He knew the garbage pick-up schedule was by 7 AM. He changed clothes to business casual; polo shirt and dark blue slacks with black dress shoes. He dumped the dusty clothes of the night before into the dumpster along with the knife he had used. He stopped and buried the pistol and extra magazines in the desert away from any traveled areas. He no longer has any evidence from the crime scene. He drives northeast towards Rodeo, New Mexico on Highway 80.

Jose Arriba joined in with a group of illegal aliens in a border crossing west of El Paso, Texas, closer to Las Cruces, New Mexico. After making the journey with the aliens looking for the 'American dream,' he separated and changed clothes in a gas station washroom. Clean dressed he will not draw the attention of officials. He walks into a buy here/pay here car lot and looks over the choices.

A salesman approaches and asks, "Can I help you today. We have an excellent choice of used beauties. You chose the perfect day because we have some limited time specials that I can give you. Have you bought from us before?"

"No, I was looking at the maroon Honda Odyssey."

"What a smart choice. You know your cars. This van is the cleanest one you will find for hundreds of miles."

As the salesman continued with his pitch, Jose listened and looked over the van. He already knew used vans of any type were rare along the border. Cartel's buy them all for use in the human smuggling operations.

"Can I get your name sir?" The salesman asked.

Jose, who by now had blocked him out looked up because he had stopped talking.

"Can I get your name sir?" The salesman repeated.

"Javier. Javier Sanchez."

Jose changed his identity before crossing and had his passport and driver's license in the new name.

"Well Javier, you certainly do have a keen eye for good cars. You have chosen the best car on the lot."

Jose knows the salesman is putting on his act, but he also knows he has to play along. He does not want this man to remember him as anything but ordinary if at all.

Jose responded, "I have worked with my father and brothers my whole life on cars and think I do know something good when I see it. You know of course I will have to look it over and take it for a test ride."

"Why of course!" The salesman said with more excitement in his voice with the thought of selling another car this week from his lot of junk. He could see that Javier knew nothing about cars and would not be on his lot if he had good credit. The shark circled the scented water with enthusiasm. If he only knew who between the two of them was the predator.

Jose test drove the van with the salesman before paying the asking price. He drove into town and checked into the Fairfield Inn paying with cash and using a different identity as planned. If things go wrong, they did not want the same name traced to all the stops. For Jose, Javier Sanchez was the identity of an old friend and all records of that identity disposed of. He is now Juan Hernandez. He asked the clerk if a package had arrived for him.

"One moment Mr. Hernandez, let me look in the back."

The clerk returned in less than 30 seconds and said, "Yes you do Mr. Hernandez. You have received a FedEx package."

He gave him the envelope that arrived that morning. He thanks the desk clerk and takes it to his room and opens it. Inside he finds a Sudoku book and a key with the number "127". Sudoku is a puzzle book using the numbers 1-9 to solve each 3x3 puzzle. He went through the book and finds what he was looking for. Within the scribbled numbers on page 91 was the symbol:

Pedro Gomez is working on a shrimp boat out of Corpus Christi, Texas. He is an experienced boat Captain and running the 47-foot Shrimp Trawler named *Mary Beth* for the owner he met six months earlier. He signed on as a deck hand but made sure everyone was aware that he has his Captains license. He has captained several other fishing vessels in Central and South America. Pedro went to visit Captain Joe Cassels at his home.

"Pedro. Come on in." Captain Cassels said as Pedro came in the apartment.

"Thank you, Captain. I hope I am not interrupting anything."

"No No. What's up?"

"I have some issues and I was wondering if we could take a drive to the docks to discuss them."

"Ok. You can't talk to me here?"

"No. I also need to show you something I think may be an issue."

"Like what?"

"I show you Captain. Cannot explain it correct like you know."

"Ok. Let me grab my shoes."

They walked out to Pedro's truck and climbed in.

Captain Cassels did not show up to work for the rest of the week angering the boat owner. It is not like Captain Joe Cassels not to show up without calling. He did have an old habit of liking liquor. His friends assumed that it is this old friend who found him again and he was too ashamed to return. His apartment was paid in advance but there was no sign of Joe.

Placed into a bad predicament, the owner heard about Pedro. Pedro smiled for a multitude of reasons as he took over as the boats captain. It will be on a trial basis at first and then full time after a week if he is as good as he claims. It was during this week that Joe Cassels apartment was emptied. It appears he has moved away. It is a tough business and these things happen. Most owners run their own boats, but Kurt Johnson is older and wants to spend more time on shore. He felt fortunate to have a man like Pedro Gomez step up to the plate and take over the boat operations.

Pedro was told from Venezuela that he would receive instructions one day by mail indicating the start of the operation. Earlier in the week before visiting Captain Cassels, he received a letter with a familiar return address from El Paso, Texas. He opened it and saw the symbol:

He knows the operation is starting and time to initiate his plans.

Each man, Tomas, Pedro, and Jose each looked at their individual message. Through their training, they knew what it meant. They were required to memorize a secret code that seemed so simple yet not detectable by law enforcement officers they may encounter. The United States depends on local, county, state, and federal law enforcement agencies to protect their citizens. Each of these agencies can be an effective defensive and offensive force if they made the effort to work together. Yet due to interagency struggles, jealousies, jurisdictional concerns, re-election ideas, and media headline captures, none of them ever work together.

Most people who encounter the police do so in a traffic stop. Their Hezbollah and Venezuelan trainers know this and had prepared the code to use for the operation. It has succeeded before on other small missions in America and they will continue its use until discovered. When seen by police officers it appears as a word game.

Looking at the code you see:

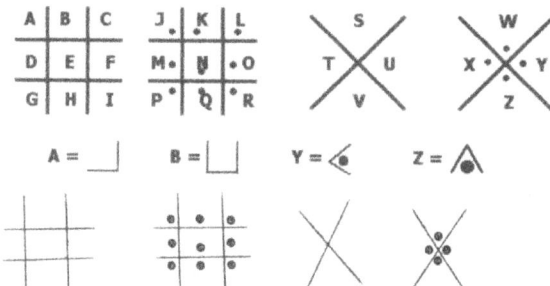

The code is a pigpen or Masonic code because of its early use with the Freemasons. It is a geometric cipher substituting letters or symbols within a grid. Any combination of letters can be placed within the grids. Anyone can decipher the words from the symbols once the key is known. Each operative remembered the code while in Venezuela. We often lose cognitive skills when we are under any type of stressful situation. Therefore, they practiced daily under various situations. Somewhere in their journey to the United States, they would each receive codes via different methods. It could be within a book, a letter, an email, or any other type of communication.

To a professional in cryptanalysis, the pigpen cipher is simplistic, but the puzzle key must be known. However, to the average person who never studies codes, it looks like a game. Sudoku books are a favorite method along with small bibles. The operative can receive a book, find the code spread throughout the book and know their next assignment. This eliminates the off chance of an electronic interception that the American Intelligence community depends. The difficulty for the Americans is an attack in an unconventional method. Simplistic measures are often overlooked. Breaking away from the Cold War mentality with the Soviets has been hard.

The code that each operative remembered was:

With the placement of the letters within the geometric shapes, they each looked at the papers and smiled.

The first symbol coincides with the geometric pattern of the third graph > without the dot inside so it is the letter "T". The next pattern is a reversed "L" without a dot and is the letter "A". The next is a reversed "C" with a dot and is found in the second chart as the letter "M". The next is also from the second chart with a dot and equates to the letter "P". The last pattern is the same as the second and is again the letter "A".

These symbols said one thing to each person; "Tampa." It can only be Tampa, Florida. Home to so many targets fresh for the picking. These targets are both soft and hard. There are malls and sporting venues where people gather by the thousands in one location. There is Mac Dill Air Force Base, home to Central Command, the brain center for the wars in the Middle East. They each thought about it and knew they need to arrive in Tampa within a week by whatever means necessary. This separation and lack of each other's plans prevents all of them from capture at the same time or information loss if one is caught.

Tomas has a second code.

With the placement of the letters to the symbols from memory, the symbol spelled the word, "Greyhound". They were to meet in Tampa, Florida at a place chosen as Greyhound. Tomas knows it is the bus station because Jose is to give him the key when they meet.

# 13

Peter too had to step over and get a cup of coffee to think this one over. Why would a drug smuggler kill two U.S. Border Patrol agents and not go back to Mexico? At least there he will be immune from government prosecution. The Mexican government will agree to extradition only if the American government puts enough pressure or to gain something they want in return. Others may refer to him as a hero for eliminating two "pinche rinche" American cops. Payments to the authorities can achieve a pass if well connected. The cartel would kill him or bargain a foothold with the Mexican authorities to turn him over if given the opportunity. Besides, he is just another mule. They are a dime for three dozen in Mexico.

Peter asked, "What about ballistics or other evidence? Do we have info on the knife, so we can look for knife type, forensics, fibers, and fingerprints? Did the killer have different footprints when he left the scene as compared to walking in?"

"Different footprints?" Sarah asked turning her head towards him and squinting her eyes. "What are you looking for there, if he changed his shoes?"

"No, I am talking about the depth of his prints. Was he walking in heavier than when he left? This will tell us he was carrying something in that he did not take back. If he was a drug mule, he could carry drugs fashioned onto his back like a backpack. These can be anywhere from 50-100 pounds depending on the strength of the mule and the distance they must walk. Also, are you saying that there was only one person? Only a single set of tracks?"

"Other than it tells us there was only one person, where is that information going in your head?" John asked.

From the back of the room, Eddie spoke up. "It tells us that this is not going to be a mule. They rarely travel alone because it makes the size of the contraband too small and not as profitable. Furthermore, if the authorities spot them with a divided load, some may get through. It is the all of the eggs in one basket philosophy."

"Exactly." Peter responded. "Often, they will hide the drugs somewhere and hope the authorities don't find it. Then they can come back later and pick it up."

The phone rang and Sarah reached over and picked it up. Peter saw her turn around and speak but could not hear what she said.

She hung up and said, "Got a call from our source in Arizona; the caliber bullet removed from the Agent they think is a 9mm. They are sending it out for forensics."

"Did you put a rush on it?" Rafael asked.

"Yes, and asked for any other information including what Peter inquired about. They said they would stay put and pass it along as it comes in. What do you think Peter?" Sarah asked.

"I'll tell you when all of the information comes in."

# 14

The next morning, Jose Arriba, aka Juan Hernandez woke early, showered, and dressed. He walked to the lobby and had the continental breakfast and scanned the news. All the channels were covering the same headline; "Two Border Patrol Agents found dead in desert." He watched the news and read the newspapers. The reports said the same thing. Jose listened to the local news reporter on television while he ate breakfast.

"Sources report that two Border Patrol agents were murdered sometimes during the night. Authorities are not releasing their identities until the next of kin are notified. Police are tight lipped about how many suspects are involved. It is unknown if this was drug violence spilling over into the United States or how the agents were murdered. As soon as we learn more, we will pass it on to you. This is Mary Cárdenas reporting from the United States Border Patrol office in Douglas, Arizona."

Jose listened as the television station brought on several so-called experts to discuss the event. They all said that this has all the signs of cartel and drug related violence. They said the suspects fled back into Mexico. With the state of relations between our countries, extradition will be slow if at all. Jose knew who the suspect was because of the timing and he awaited more information.

Tomas drove through Rodeo and continued north to Interstate 10 and then traveled west to Lordsburg, New Mexico. He exited onto Main Street and traveled north to Motel Drive stopping at his chosen hotel for the night; the American Hotel.

"I like the irony of names and missions." He thought to himself.

Now he awaits his next message arriving by text. It came the next morning as are millions of texts that time of day around the country. Designed to blend in with all the other traffic and use simple language, it avoids the technology driven security of the American government.

"Meet you for breakfast in the lobby."

The meet was prearranged, and the text was for security. Tomas already knew where to go and he now knows Jose completed his journey. He packed his belongings and checked out of the hotel. He smiles pulling out of the parking lot and re-enters Interstate 10 driving east. Las Cruces is only 120 miles away. He will arrive in 2 hours.

Pedro had received a bible with the same code as the others and knows it's time to start the plan. He was closer, but because of his travel means knew he would need to start soon. He was going to Captain a boat to Florida. This arrangement was put in place early in the planning and the reason he is in Corpus. He needs at least two other crewmembers to run the net trawls and separate the fish caught in the nets if this was a normal trip. The crews of these vessels are not dependable and often move around. Many crew members use shrimping as a temporary job until other work arrives. However, since hurricanes Katrina and Rita devastated the gulf coast region in 2005, many of the crews came from Mexico. Workers are needed and the Mexican migration into the gulf coast region is intense.

On this morning Pedro made sure that the only crewmember who showed up for work was Sani. Sani was short for Sandival and is an older Mexican man with no family and few friends. He always shows up when called and works hard. Manual, the other younger man was at home with his family when he received a call from a number he did not recognize. It was a man's voice and speaking low told him in Spanish, "Immigration is coming soon. Get your family and leave."

Startled, Manual asked, "Who is this?"

The voice said, "A friend."

Manual turns to his wife and says, "Pack everything, we are leaving."

Pedro hangs up the public pay phone at the convenience store and walks back to his truck. He removes his cell phone and calls Kurt Johnson, the boat owner.

"Hola jefe, this is Pedro."

"Hey Pedro, how are things. Everybody there? You going out today?"

"Yes jefe. We are going out today, but Manual has not shown up and I tried to call him. There is no answer."

"That's strange. Manual always shows up on time. Was he sick yesterday?"

"No jefe, I do not know. Sani and I could use some help and I want to ask if you want to come today. It has been a while, and you should always spend some time out."

"First Joe and now Manuel! What in the hell is happening?"

Kurt Johnson had not been out on the boat and was trying to stay busy. His kids were away in college and his wife, Mary Beth, was lost to breast cancer five years before. He thought it would be good to go out with his wife's namesake again and said, "Sure Pedro, I will get my stuff together."

"This is good jefe. I will get the boat ready."

Pedro was pleased at how well this was coming together.

# 15

The call came into the office that night with more forensic information involving the murders. Peter was driving home. He lives alone in a condominium in south Miami. He had been involved in several relationships, none lasting for long. The type of service he performed in the military wreaked havoc on any chance of a normal homelife. You must be there to nurture. He once had a cat even though he preferred dogs. Cats can last for days with a large bowl of water and food and litter. Still, someone needs to appear to maintain these.

The training and type of work he performs never turns off. Survival means always staying on his a-game. In Delta, part of their training was to dress to blend into the area. They learned surveillance and counter surveillance techniques, how to arrange drop locations and gather intelligence along with SERE or Survival, Evade, Resist, and Escape techniques. He watches his mirrors for vehicles he recognizes from other roads and never takes the same route home. He uses a turn signal and slows then turns the other way or makes a U-turn if suspicious. These counter-surveillance techniques seem excessive, but not to Peter. He remembers the axiom; "Practice does not make perfect, only perfect practice makes perfect." Regular practice helps keep things in order in Peters mind.

He approaches his condominium and looks at cars parked along the road. Is anyone sitting in them or with tint too dark or out of state tags or rentals? He turns into his complex and looks down the street for anything suspicious. He never parks in front of his own building and always backs into his parking space. He walks to his second-floor condo and glances at the lower hinge of the door where he placed a small piece of a toothpick. If anyone had opened the door, it would fall to the ground. It was there so he entered the home. He sat for a moment when his cell phone rang.

"Hello?"

"Hey Peter, its Sarah. We received more info on ballistics. They thought it was a standard 9mm."

"Thought?"

"Yeah, but it turned out to be a 9.3mm. I did not know..."

She was cut off as Peter says, "Makarov."

"Yeah, that's what I was about to say. Not as common but not uncommon either. With the drug war across the border, they see all types of weapons from around the world. This is supposed to be some Soviet preferred weapon and used by the East Germans during the cold war. If that's true, there are probably thousands of them in Mexico."

"Ok Sarah, thanks for the call and I'll see you tomorrow."

After hanging up, Peter was thinking to himself. Odd things are coming together in this event. One person kills two well-trained and equipped agents. One is shot with a weapon of Soviet design and use. How many Makarovs are there in this hemisphere? Most weapons in the Mexican drug war are American for the simple reason of being a superpower on its border. There is no need for trans-oceanic shipments when they can drive into the United States. A Soviet preferred weapon would more likely be found in a country with direct weapon sales with the Soviets. The first that comes to mind is Iran. Could this person be Iranian? Second, it would make more sense for the person to be Iranian trained. Iranian trained in this part of the world is Venezuela. A Venezuelan enters the United States and murders two federal agents. But why? One is skillfully knifed. He was not just stabbed, he was assassinated. Surprising someone and being able to cut their throat by itself is difficult. But add to that a kidney thrust followed by a subclavian sever has professional written all over it. Knife fighting focuses on stabbing actions to reach vital areas. Slashing is superficial unless an artery is hit and is intended to psychologically disable an opponent. He waits in ambush for other agents to arrive instead of fleeing. After committing these acts, he moves towards the border, and then turns back. He is determined. The drug trade does not fit this modus operandi, but terrorism does. This person is a pro. Why is he here?

# 16

Jose Arriba is sitting in the lobby of the hotel when Tomas walks in through the glass self-opening double doors. Tomas slows to allow his eyes to focus before moving towards the breakfast lounge. He sees Jose sitting with his back to the wall on the left side of the room and away from windows and doors; a clear view of the area with no access for anyone to approach him from behind. "Good." Tomas said to himself. "He is still practicing what he was taught."

"Que Paso." Jose said aloud as Tomas approached. "How are you?"

"Well, and you?"

"Good. Would you like something to eat or drink? Help yourself."

"I am fine, are you ready? We have a lot of work to do today."

"My things are in the car."

"Good. Follow me."

Leaving the hotel, they enter their vehicles and leave the city eastbound. They arrive in El Paso, Texas an hour later. Tomas finds the address of the Wal-Mart on Gateway Boulevard W because it is open 24 hours. He drives into the parking lot and parks on the side lot across from Sam's Club. He removes his belongings and places them into Jose's van. He leaves the doors unlocked with the keys in the ignition and enters the passengers' door of the van and said, "Let's go."

Jose drives to Interstate 10 and enters the freeway eastbound. The plan is progressing. They know the car will end up stolen and in Mexico in short order. The rental is in someone else's name, so Tomas doesn't worry about the return.

He looks at Jose and ask, "Do you have the key?"

"Yes." He removed it from his pocket and gave it to Tomas who asked, "Have you heard anything from Pedro and Humberto?"

"I got a text from Pedro that he was leaving as scheduled, but nothing from Humberto."

Tomas did not say anything, but he dislikes loose ends.

"Humberto had better have a damn good excuse. If not, I will kill him myself."

Humberto Santos is the third member of their trained team and the fourth member of the group. He was to cross further west on the border and start his journey.

Kurt Johnson and Sani meet Pedro at the docks that afternoon. Pedro was on board the *Mary Beth* and helps the excited owner stow his bags in the bunkhouse. Pedro went shopping earlier in the day and supplied the boat for the three of them for a week and paid on the business account. Pedro knew he might need the extra supplies later if all went well. After storing the gear and topping off the tanks, he hollers for Sani to pull the ropes. Ropes stored on board, the *Mary Beth* with Captain Pedro and deck hands, Sani and Kurt head into the Gulf. He brings the boat up to cruising speed and travels east by southeast. The rest of the crew is unaware that the current destination was over 800 miles away. Everyone who would report the boat late to the Coast Guard is on board.

Tomas and Jose travel east on Interstate 10. They dressed in casual dress clothes to give the appearance of business travelers if observed by police officers.

"I am glad to see you have not added tint to the windows." Tomas said.

"No, I can always do that later if our needs change."

"Be sure to drive the speed limit and watch for any construction and speed limit changes. We don't have anything, but we do not want our information in any police data base."

"Do you know anything else other than the location?"

"No. You will know what you need when it is time for you to know." Tomas said in a tone that inflected his feelings of "don't ask me these questions" attitude. Jose understood and did not ask again.

They approached their first obstacle and had discussed it during their drive; the Sierra Blanca checkpoint. The Sierra Blanca is an interior permanent Border Patrol checkpoint on Interstate 10. All east-west traffic must slow for inspection. According to the U.S. General Accounting Office, these checkpoints are "the third layer in the Border Patrol's three-layer strategy," following "line watch" and "roving patrol" operations near the border. Checkpoints are placed on primary border roads to deter illegal alien and smuggling operations. Even though they are found up to 75 miles inland from the border, due to their border connection, they still require everyone to stop for inspection. There are also Tactical checkpoints on roadways used by travelers attempting to by-pass the permanent stations.

Tomas said, "Just drive normal and slow down enough to stop if needed. Remember not to get nervous because even if they search us, there is nothing to find. As we get closer start telling me a story about football."

"What? About football?"

"Yes, football. I want to hear your best story. One that will make me laugh and do not stop telling me unless we are stopped."

They approached the inspecting agent and Jose starts talking about the whores of Caracas. A surprised Tomas smiles and laughs. Juan waves at the agent who slowed them with a hand signal. The Border Patrol agent can see two Hispanic men in business casual clothes. They appear to be conversing and laughing as they approach. Showing no nervous signs, he waves them through. Tomas thought about how that agent will never know he waved on the killer of his co–workers.

"What did you do that for?" Tomas asked.

"You stated they were looking for unusual behaviors in people and to act like nothing was wrong."

"I said talk about football, not whores."

"Who laughed loudest, me or you?"

Tomas smiled again and let it pass.

The *Mary Beth* is about 100 miles from port by sunset. Kurt is below making supper. The cook's job was often performed by one of the other men, but Kurt insisted. Pedro looks out at the horizon in every direction and watches his radar screen. He sees the lights of other boats in the area but only one shows up on radar that scans 10 miles around the shrimp trawler. Pedro smells a roast cooking. The smell of beef, onion, garlic, and herbs drifts through the interior of the boat. Sani is on the rear deck examining the nets for holes and sewing them when found.

Kurt also made steamed asparagus and a mixture of red potatoes, carrots, and onions drizzled with olive oil and Italian seasoning. He calls out to the others when the dinners ready, and they all move to the captains' wheelhouse. Pedro and Sani step in and smile when they see the plates.

Kurt tells them, "I wanted to cook a grand meal for you boys before we start, to show my appreciation to all your hard work."

"Here, here!" Pedro and Sani said almost in unison as they held up their Coke cans.

"To the start of a great shrimping week." Kurt says as he glances at the GPS navigation.

"Hey Pedro, aren't we kinda far out to the southeast?"

"Don't worry jefe, I have good information where the shrimp are."

Kurt smiled, "You're a good Captain, Pedro."

They all began to devour their plates and sharing some small talk. The night signals the start of shrimping.

# 17

Peter arrived at the office on time, but he had left his home early. He follows the same techniques to get to work used to go home. He is buzzed through the doors and walks into the office and sees John Hatfield.

"John, a word?"

"Sure, over here."

Peter follows John into a side office and says, "You get the ballistics information?"

"I did. Interesting. What are your thoughts?"

"I have been thinking this over since Sarah called last night. I don't like it."

John sat on the edge of a desk and listened. Even though Peter was the new guy, no one gets into the group unless everyone feels they are on the top of their game. Even the greenest team member is better than the most experienced in other organizations. Whenever one of them says something, they all listen.

Peter continues. "The bullet is Soviet origin. We have two agents killed. One, alright, I'll accept that someone gets off a lucky shot. But it is an unusual Soviet weapon and ammunition. Odd but possible. My problems are the first agent is not shot, not stabbed, but has his throat slit, kidney stuck, and chest drained. I say not stabbed because that is what a street thug will do. Our guy is trained. No doubt, he is the first of the two killed. He surprises him, cuts him so no one else in the area can hear a gun shot. Then, instead of fleeing south back into Mexico, he takes the time to sit and wait in ambush to kill the back-up."

John nods his head in an affirmative manner.

"Having the gun silenced makes sense to me."

"Why?"

"Because no one else in the area, even though they are far away, heard gunshots. At night, without all the background or white noise like cars, planes, etc., sound carries far. Especially in the desert where there are no buildings or other objects to reflect sound."

Peter pauses a moment and continues, "So, the perp then moves back towards the border and tries to brush his tracks, covers his shoes as he returns towards his original destination, probably Douglas. He knows by moving back towards the border, this is what a common mule or criminal will do. He doesn't have drugs. They are not valuable enough. He is zeroed in on a target or mission."

"Why Douglas and risk returning to the U.S.?"

"It is the only town in reach big enough to not attract attention to a stranger. Something else was in play or happened to give him enough confidence to try again to move north. I have made some calls to confirm this idea. His target..."

John interrupts him. "Target?"

"Yeah, target is not Douglas, but is somewhere he needs to be to continue to his destination."

"And where is that?"

"Don't know. Don't know target, numbers, associates, mission or anything else. I do know this; he is not a mule, alien looking for work, or another common border issue. Also, I would bet that he is not Mexican." This caused a micro expression on John's face. Micro expressions are slight muscle twitches showing a reaction to information received.

"And why is that?"

"The weapon used is a Makarov. Not an uncommon weapon but uncommon in this hemisphere. Yes, I know the AK47 is popular in the Mexican drug war, but they are Romanian manufactured when bought in the United States."

Peter stops a moment to collect his thoughts and continues.

"We have to think Soviet or Chinese equipment being used where and then connected to South America. The Iranians have a lot of trade with both the Russians and the Chinese with fuel. They receive military aid from those countries. Iran in turn sponsors terrorism and supports the socialist government of Venezuela. They also help to train the FARC rebels in Columbia who are responsible for countless acts of terrorism. The Iran Republican Guard also trains operatives and troops in Venezuela. What if, and I say this carefully, what if this person is an Iranian trained Venezuelan entering the United States to coordinate some type of terrorist attack?"

John sat for a moment before asking, "Why would he have to be a terrorist? Why not a spy?"

"Easy, a spy would not come here armed to the teeth and risk capture transporting weapons across the border. A terrorist would."

John stood up and said, "I like it. It sounds feasible. Justice is still looking at it as a panicked drug smuggler over reacting. We are still on the fringes and watching the developments. We have several other events happening around the world we are monitoring as well. We will intercede at the point that we can show a credible threat. I'll take it up the chain. One question though. Suggestions on how we find out where, who, how many or even to confirm your theory?"

Peter has thought about this already and responds, "Yes, check surveillance cameras in the Douglas area for the hours before sunrise on the day of the incident. Check information on stolen or rented vehicles in that area as well. Also have the

Border Patrol check to see if they arrested any OTM's (Other Than Mexicans) before or after in that sector."

John walked out. Peter thought longer of his ideas and if there was anything he was missing. He felt strong about this and his sixth senses were screaming that something was happening.

He received a text that read, "Regarding info you requested about the events the night of the murders. They were operating a skeleton crew due to an unusually large increase in crossings in that area and further west."

He went to tell John. The extra movements may have been intentional to open the area for this person to get through undetected. His theory is becoming a truth.

# 18

Humberto Santos is the third member of the team from Venezuela and fourth in the group. Except for Tomas, they each entered the country with little information about the other members locations and new names. Humberto is the youngest assigned to the mission. Pedro, the boat captain is the oldest, has no living family and has worked in various positions for the government. His age and smile are deceiving. He has killed for the sake of killing and has no remorse.

Humberto was forced to train as a soldier. As a conscript of the party's Special Unit squad, he was raised in a reform school and never liked authority. He views it as those with the legal power to hurt others. He never likes being on the receiving end of authority but agreed to become a part of it to avoid the punishments for not joining. He is a good operative but not with his heart as are the others.

Jose has known Tomas for several years. He is a competent operator having assisted him on missions in the past. When Tomas was assigned to oversee this operation, the largest and boldest of its kind, he at once chose Jose as his second in command. He was familiar with the work of Pedro and knew he was a loyal soldier but lacked the skills needed to lead. Humberto is an unknown and he does not like unknowns. He studied Humberto's records after he was selected from the Venezuelan military. Tomas had the ability to remove their selection especially someone this young. He had his reasons for keeping him. Events can arise when he needs someone young or expendable. Sacrificing Jose or Pedro is a last resort scenario. As such, Humberto had less information than the others.

Tomas, like Pedro, has worked for the government for a long time. He once met Cuban President Fidel Castro during his many visits to Venezuela and was captivated with his confidence of power. He trained for years to carry out secret missions for the government, both inside and out of the country. Political parties who challenge the authority of dictatorship in Venezuela often find themselves in precarious positions. Tomas has helped the government in the elimination of several party members. He is a dangerous man, killing by any means necessary. It is second nature to him. He is loyal to the dictator and chosen to lead this operation.

Humberto Santos has higher expectations of his abilities than the others placed on him. He is the low man on the proverbial totem pole. He felt his past assignments were below his skills set and was disappointed that no matter how much he did for the government, others were rewarded. Once again, he must take orders from everyone involved in this mission. He has a job to do but is getting tired of the disrespect.

"Someday." He thought to himself. "I will use my skills and monies to go to America and stay."

He has been here several times before to collect information on various industries. "Surely my skills would be more appreciated by the Americans."

"Hey, pendejo!" the Mexican coyote hollered. "Quit daydreaming and let's move. The sun is almost down."

Humberto had to cross the border as a regular Mexican laborer and was not given as much money as the others. He saw this as another sign of disrespect to his abilities. Tomas and Jose had taken the bulk of the monies and told Humberto to cross over and buy a cheap car or catch a bus. More money will be available after reaching his destination. Here he is living in the desert with Mexican aliens suffering at the hands of another asshole 17-year-old smuggler who thinks he is a big shot. He is in the eyes of the others, but not Humberto. He plans to kill him if he ever gets the chance. The group is mostly women, one that has a small child.

The coyote leads the group of aliens to the border fence east of Douglas, Arizona. The location is further to the west where the coyote said he has been many times. They could try to cross at other locations but going alone increased the chances of capture by the Border Patrol. Besides, if caught, they would be detained, identified, and deported across the border, so they could try again. Many of these coyotes are ruthless. They care little for the souls they guide and look for only the money the business provides. Robberies and rapes are common along the border, but still they come north.

They can see lights shining from homes and businesses in the distance. The fence, three strands of stretched wire is all that separated them from the United States. The coyote held up the fence strands and kept repeating, "Keep walking straight ahead. Don't stop unless I tell you to."

The last person passes and follows the one ahead in single file. Walking a short distance into the United States the coyote, who stayed in the rear of the group yells in Spanish, "Immigration, run away! Run away!" The group runs to the north as instructed. Humberto starts to run and stops in the dark. All his senses on high alert. He kneels on one knee and looks back to see if he sees their coyote. Instead, he hears him laughing as he trots back to Mexico.

He thinks to himself, "I have to stay calm."

His training is taking over. His instructor told him in Venezuela that in moments like this, you must remember the CPR classes. He can still hear the instructor telling them, "When a situation arises fast, you need to react fast. Response by itself is not enough. It must be the right action. How do you find the right response? First, evaluate the scene. Is it life threatening to you or one of your comrades? Then, and only then, will it be necessary to take whatever action is needed to eliminate the threat. If it is not, the easiest way to remember what to do is CPR. I know each of you has that look on your face, what are you talking about, Cardiopulmonary Resuscitation? What do you do before you start CPR; look, listen, and feel. That is what I want you do when a situation of surprise that is not life threatening occurs. Relax by calming your breathing. If you are in an intense situation, the worst thing you can do is panic. Keep your head clear so you can evaluate and respond. Look around, move to a position of cover, and evaluate. Listen to the activities around you and a solution will come. Feel for your equipment and available weapons or use this moment to determine how to respond. You may believe that all this could take too long. I can assure you that by the time I am finished, you will react to any situation. The repetition applied will help you to respond and not sit and think. You will be surprised at how fast you will react once the situation is known."

Kneeling in the dark desert, Humberto realizes his money is stolen. They each had paid $2000.00 up front for the guided service. Not that any of these people care about the welfare of their clients, but most will at least try to get you where they say. To take your money and leave you behind like this is life threatening. These people have spent a year or more saving for this trip.

He redirects his focus towards the others. He hears them running. They started out in the same direction, but soon became separated. He knew he did not want to move in the same area as the rest of them. The likelihood of drawing unwanted attention is too great. He never saw or heard the immigration agents. He has a fighting knife in his back waistband and a pistol in the front. He is deciding if he should run back to Mexico or toss the weapons. It is a set-up, so he stands. He is close enough and has his night vision intact from the last hour in the dark. It is not the best decision, but he takes it anyway. He runs to the south, crosses back into Mexico and sees the coyote ahead. He pretends to be respectful.

"Señor! Señor!" He said in a hushed voice.

"Un momento por favor Señor."

The coyote looks back surprised. "Que paso pendejo! What are you doing? I cannot take you back over the fence without another payment."

"I understand but there was no Immigration."

"What are you saying! I was lying! Do you know who you are talking to! Fuck you. I will not take you back in either direction."

"You sent all those women and a child running in the desert and left them."

"Fuck you. I will see to you when I get back."

"See to me now."

Humberto reached out and grabbed the teen by his hair and yanked him forward and down. At the same time, he brought up his right knee and contacted the boys' nose. He felt it shatter and flatten and the teen moaned as he reached for his face. Humberto placed him into a bilateral neck restraint with his right arm and locked it in with his left. The teen struggled, kicking his feet but to no avail. It took a few seconds longer for him to pass out without receiving blood to the brain.

"Must be your adrenaline. Relax. Go to sleep. Pendejo!" Humberto said to the teen. "I hope you were alive long enough to hear that."

Humberto held the lock for a little longer before removing his knife and stabbing him in the neck. This will assure the teen is dead. He moves back to the fence and waits. Still no sounds or lights of the Border Patrol. He re-crosses into America and walks towards the northeast. Turning north, the eastern lean in the direction of travel vectored him far away from the others.

Humberto is moving slow through the desert terrain. Confidence again flows through him. The rest of the group is separated by at least a mile. His actions were based on emotion and not logic by going back into Mexico. The detour south cost him time and distance. His trainers would tell him that he risked the operation for personal reasons.

"It's true." He thought to himself. "I lost it a moment. But it felt good. Besides, the others attracted any border agents within miles. They had to set off every sensor in the valley."

He sat for a moment to catch his breath and have a drink of water. A twig snapped to his left and startled him. Was it a sound of an animal or something else? There is no way it could be any part of the group because they had all ran to the north and west. He stops breathing for a moment and listens. He cannot see far in the brush. There were shadows from the moon light and the internal pounding of his heartbeat is louder than the environment.

Humberto sat motionless for five minutes. It felt like five hours. There were no other sounds as he rises and moves again. His gait cautious as the confidence he had moments earlier faded. Out of the dark a bright light came on causing him to hold his hands up to shield his eyes and he turns to run.

"Alto. Alto, Policia Inmigration. He's running southwest!" The voice yells out.

Humberto panics and runs into a bush having lost his night vision cutting his arms, face, and neck.

He stumbles as he hears another voice to his right yell, "I got him Clay, over here."

Then as fast as he started, something large slams into him from his left forward angle sending him flying backwards into the desert floor.

"I got him." Yells the giant of a man who had performed a perfect right shoulder tackle.

Humberto chokes for air a moment and recovers as he regains some oxygen. The other Border Patrol agents ran up as Clay yells, "Damn Rick, that was the best tackle I have seen in a while. That son of a bitch never knew what hit him."

They roll him over on his stomach and had flex cuffs on his wrist before he can do anything. Rick, the former outside linebacker for Texas Tech begins a quick pat down. He grips the man tighter as the agent yells, "What the fuck do we have here."

Rick removes a 10-inch knife in the small of Humberto's back and a pistol from his front waistband. Tomas had told him to ditch his weapons if they suspected trouble. Humberto, despite the orders, was tired of the same lectures and failed when it counted. He thought about fighting back because the others would kill him for being caught. There was no way he could fight back against these three. He was arrested.

Clay took the pistol and said, "What is this? I expected some old Colt, Smith, or Taurus pistol."

He rubbed it and looked closer in the light and said, "Pistolet Besshumnyj. Sounds German or something."

Jack Jones, the third agent said, "It's a PB6P9. It's Soviet and rare in these parts. That's an old KGB pistol."

Clay looks at Humberto and said, "Vamanos, Let's go. Jack, call this in. This shithead should be investigated further. This ain't no common "wet".

# 19

Humberto is brought into the Douglas, Arizona Border Patrol sector office for processing with Mexican documentation. A fingerprint check reveals no prior arrest. The FBI is the lead for murder investigation of the two agents and the information of the identification is turned over to them. The weapons are turned over to the Bureau of Alcohol Tobacco and Firearms or ATF for processing.

In Miami, John Hatfield walks into the office and sees Peter working on a computer.

"Peter!" He says to get his attention.

He looks up. John directs him to follow with a nod of the head.

"Sarah!" John calls out.

She looks up and stands.

"Where's Rafael?"

"I'll get him." She said.

They all walk to a back room and John says, "Alright, listen up. Last night or early this morning, the Border Patrol in the same sector, Douglas sector, arrested a lone subject. He had a fighting knife and a PB6P9 Makarov pistol, and three thousand dollars U.S."

"Now were talking." Rafael interjected.

John continues, "The subject is Mexican or at least has Mexican papers. Fingerprint checks are negative. The FBI is there to interview him. They think it is possible this guy has a connection to the murders."

A snicker sounds off around the room.

"I am waiting for any documentation and fingerprint copies to arrive through Washington. No one knows we are looking at this. Peter, I like what you told me earlier. I have been bantering it around in my head. It makes sense and making sense is the first priority for me to put the pieces together."

Peter says, "I need to get out there. This guy is not going to be Mexican. We all know how easy it is in the current environment to get fake papers. Having the same weapons pop up in the same area covers my thoughts of not accepting coincidences."

"Can someone fill in the rest of us?" Sarah asked.

"I'm already on it Peter." John says and looks at Sarah. "Peter can do that on the flight. Do you have your go-bags ready?"

They all nodded.

"Good. I'm setting up a safe house over there for the work and will communicate with Sarah on the logistics."

Go-bags are a single bag with a few days change of clothes, toiletries, essentials, and tools needed to get by in case of an emergency. They never have to go pack before a last-minute trip. Every operator has one.

"Be at Miami International, the private jet sector in an hour. A jet is there prepping. I need you all out there and get a handle on this. I need this guy to talk. If anyone tries to place a roadblock, let me know. I already have calls in to D.C."

Outside, they removed their bags from their cars as a van pulled up. Jesse, another team member is driving and knew where to take them. There is no need to clear security when flying by private aircraft. Airborne, they will arrive in about four hours. Peter explains to Sarah and Rafael the details he spoke to John regarding Iranian trained Venezuelans involved in the murders and that he believes this person is in America to cause deeper harm.

"This is the reason we are looking at this. If it is nothing then we can move to our next assignment. But, if it is something bigger, we can get out in front." He then discussed what the plans will be when they arrived. "Gotta get him in our own place fast. Interrogate without the rules."

After explaining some ideas, they all chime in with information and possibilities. Peter closed his eyes and fell asleep when they finished.

The tires braking at Tucson, Arizona woke him. The others were awake and talking. The plane taxied to a hanger, stopped, and opened. They were met by an unhappy looking face.

"I don't know what the hell is going on here, I was told to meet and take you to the Tucson office." said FBI Special Agent Joe McElroy. "I am the case agent for the murders and involved in the investigation on the arrest made here. Who are you guys and why am I shuttling you to the office?"

Smiling inside Peter says, "We will talk on the way. Where's your car, we're in a hurry. Tell us what you know so far."

This attitude frosted him more, but he was told to cooperate by his superiors.

"Again. Who are you?"

Peter looked him dead in the eyes and said, "Listen McElroy, I can appreciate the fact that your mad. I can appreciate the fact that you care enough to get mad. All that I can say is we are on the same team. Let's work together and cooperate and we will be gone."

Agent McElroy stood silently a moment, turned and walked towards the Chevy SUV. They all followed and climbed in. Peter started the conversation.

"I see the prisoner was already transferred out of Douglas. Has he said anything?"

"No, other than the general pedigree information. Said he is from Mexico. We have sent the Mexican authorities his information and awaiting a response. His paperwork identifies him as Humberto Santos. Probably a fake name."

"Good luck with that one." Peter replied in response to waiting for Mexico to cooperate.

As they arrived at the Federal building, they park in the back and enter through various security points until they arrive at the interrogation room.

"That's all Joe. Thanks for all you did. We will take it from here. Also, we will be taking him with us."

SA McElroy looked up and said, "Oh no you don't. This is still my prisoner!"

Before he could say another word, Peter interrupted. "I thought you and I were told that we would have your full assistance."

"Well, well you..."

"That's what I thought. Call your boss, call your wife, call whoever, and again, thanks for the help."

SA McElroy stared at him for a moment and turned down the hallway and pulled out his cell phone.

Rafael said, "Peter you're being a little tough with the guy. We really are on the same team."

Peter looked at him and said, "I know you've worked with the Bureau before."

"Yeah. But. Never mind." Rafael says smiling.

Sarah, on the phone hangs up and says, "Ok. Everything is lined up. We got our place."

They enter the room and see Humberto sitting behind a desk, drinking a Coke with an empty McDonald's bag next to him. Peter walks up to him, grabs his left arm and said, "You're going with us."

Humberto said smugly, "Finally, I am going back to the border. I will need to get home."

Peter looked at him and said, "Good you speak English. Don't count on going home."

# 20

The kitchen and dining table was cleaned after dinner. Before going back in the wheelhouse of the *Mary Beth*, Pedro asked Sani to fill two five-gallon buckets of chum and set them near the back deck.

"Chum? What for. We have never used chum before."

"I am testing a theory and think we will get extra fish with the shrimp. I brought cow's blood from the butcher store and mixed it with cut up trash fish. It is in the cooler on the deck."

Sani nodded his head and went back to the rear deck mumbling, "Sharks maybe, but for shrimp? You're the capitano!"

Kurt asked Pedro if all was ok and after getting a "thumbs up" said, "I'm going
to hit the sack for a while. I'll relieve you in a few hours."

"Thanks, jefe, sounds good."

Pedro set the autopilot of the vessel to keep the boat on the designated course. He checks the radar again and there are no other boats close by, so he goes below and walks to the back deck. Sani is sitting on the edge watching the chlorophyll fluorescence in the water created by the plankton stirred by the propellers. It leaves a greenish hue in the water along the trail of the boat seen from above.

"Que paso mi amigo. Are those the buckets of chum?" Pedro called out to Sani looking at the five-gallon buckets on the starboard rear deck.

"Hola El Capitan. Si. Filled as you instructed"

"Good. Thank you."

"How are the nets?"

"I found a few tears but they are fixed now."

Pedro smiled and nodded.

"You doing alright Sani?"

"Si, just watching the evening and thinking about home."

"What do you see when you look out there?"

Sani turned to glance out over the stern and is struck hard in the head. He glances back and sees a blurred image of Pedro standing with a fish Billy Club. The club looks like a small baseball bat and is used to stun fish to keep them from damaging the boats interior when pulled onto the deck. Then all went black as blood flowed out of his wound. Pedro grabs him to keep him from falling into the gulf and making a splash. This could bring Kurt to the deck before he was ready. He held him under his armpits and eased him into the water. He watched as the limp human form with arms and black hair floated out to the sides and faded into the darkness of the night. He grabs a five-gallon bucket of chum and pours it into the water. He smiles and returns to the wheelhouse.

A couple of hours later, Kurt climbs into the wheelhouse holding a big black and hot cup of coffee. Pedro looks over and smiles.

"Morning jefe, feel better?"

"Yes, I do Pedro. Quite honestly, I did not want to wake up. I have always slept well with the motions of the boat at sea. Funny thing though, I had the strangest dream about Mary Beth. It was as if she was right here with me. Where's Sani?"

"Don't know. Last time I saw him was at the back deck." He said with a grin. In his mind, he says, "At least I am not lying to the boss."

"He wasn't in his bunk and I glanced out back and didn't see him there either. Thought maybe he was up here with you."

"I'm sure it's nothing boss, let's go look again."

He set the boat on autopilot and follows Kurt down to the deck. They walk outside and moved to the aft or back of the boat. Kurt sat his coffee down on the wooden bait-cutting box and yells "Sani!"

At this moment, a blinding pain flew through his body causing him to arch backwards. The pain is so intense that he cannot speak. Pedro stands behind him with a filet knife driven into his kidney and left there a moment. The response allows him to reach up, grab Kurt's chin, and twist his head to the left. He removes the knife from his lower back and drags the blade across his throat and side of his neck. Without a sound he slides the body off the back of the boat. He grabs the second five-gallon bucket of chum and pours it over the side. He picks up Kurt's cup of coffee and walks back to the wheelhouse. He said aloud to the gulf waters churning with chlorophyll fluorescence in the water created by the plankton and stirred by the propellers, "Say hello to Mary Beth."

He looks up the coordinates to the Tampa Bay shipping channel and enters them into his autopilot.

# 21

Without saying anything until the time was right, Peter, Sarah, and Rafael drove Humberto to a safe house John and Sarah had arranged for unrestricted access. They arrive and stop in the driveway. The garage door opens and they pull in as the door closes.

Humberto looking around says. "What's going on? Where are we? Why haven't I been released yet?"

"You will after a short pit stop." Peter responded.

They went inside where they found team analyst Pat Young and George Wilcox.

"You can take him back there." Pat said looking up from her computer screen and pointing to a door on the other side of the room. "The gear is set up."

Peter looks around and sees secure satellite phones and four computers at various locations. "Impressive." He said a loud, but no one answered.

Humberto, feeling anxious starts to push back. Peter hit him in the base of his neck lightly and said, "Keep moving."

"What the fuck is going on here? Who are you?"

Peter responds as they enter a bedroom, "People have been asking that question a lot lately. Sit down in that chair."

There was no other furniture. Humberto sat as they duct taped his arms and legs to the chair.

"Wait, what are you doing? I don't know anything about anything. I'm trying to find work. What are you doing? I don't know anything about drugs, please!"

Sarah sat outside and started going through the paperwork from the file they received from the FBI. The gun and knife were entered into evidence in Douglas by the ATF and the gun is being sent to Washington in the morning for ballistics testing.

Peter with Rafael behind him looks at Humberto and said, "What can you tell about the murders of the border patrol agents?"

Humberto looks at him and said, "Murders? Señor, I did not kill anybody. I do not know what you are talking about."

He explained how the group was held for an extra day in Mexico at a halfway house awaiting transportation. This information is verifiable with sources meaning he may have an alibi. All they were told by their coyotes was there had been extra activity the day before on the U.S. side. Now Humberto suspected why; Tomas.

"Serious señor, I don't know nothing."

Peter was watching for any micro expressions which would show anything different. When you tell fabricated stories, little expressions give it away. Peter saw none. He did notice the slight hesitation and knew he was thinking.

"Alright Bert, if you didn't do it, who did?"

"I don't know señor, I swear. I do not know what you are talking about."

"Listen Bert," a nickname Peter used to see if it upset him. "You may not have been there, and I have to tell you that if true, extends your life expectancy. However, you know who did. In fact, I watched you look at his picture a moment ago in your mind."

"I saw no pictures señor!"

Peter understands the Interviewing and Interrogation skill of Neurolinguistics to verify a person is trying to answer the question truthfully. He is watching Humberto's eyes after baselining what is normal, he can see that he answers questions the same as he did during non-threatening questions.

"That pistol you had…"

Humberto interrupts, "I found that in the desert, señor and the knife. The desert is full of trash left over from smugglers and people. Honest I don't know anything."

"You're lying Bert, and you're not from Mexico."

He took a stab at his theory and said, "You're Venezuelan."

As he said it, he saw it. A slight lip twinge that said he was on the right path. If he believed, and he did, that Humberto had not killed the agents then this means there are more of them.

"My question is why are you all here and where are you going."

The question caused a slight reaction and he now knew there were more of them.

There was a knock at the door and it opened. Sarah looked in and said, "Can I see you a moment?" Peter looked at Rafael to continue the pressure and walked out the door.

"I found this in a small bible in his belongings."

"What is it, hieroglyphics?"

"I don't know, but it was drawn in the front cover."

"That could be scribbling or someone else's scribbling. What else is there?"

"That's just it!" Sarah said. "There isn't anything else."

"That's all we got?"

That's what I'm telling you. There is nothing else written anywhere. There are no scribblings and the bible is new. Every personal bible I've seen is well used with passages marked. This is something either he wrote in there or someone gave it to him already inscribed. No way is he a doodler on one thing and writing nothing anywhere else. He's too clean."

Peter says, "Does it look like anything to you and the others?"

"I believe it's something. This guy is no standard alien. There are none of the common mannerisms and he did not have the normal items with him when he was caught."

"Like?"

"Like, water. They all carry milk jugs of water. Maybe he dropped it when the Border Patrol gave chase." Sarah said.

"I read the report. They never chased him and he was a mile away from where the others were found. He may have crossed with the group and went a different direction. Can I hang on to this a moment?"

"Yep. We photographed it and the others are looking into it."

Peter took the bible and returned to the room. Rafael was in his face and talking in Spanish. Peter opened the bible and handed it to Rafael. Humberto looked up and Peter saw his eye pupils expand. A normal expression when you see something that excites or surprises you. Peter knew they were on the right path if we can make him talk. This is easier without rules than many realize. He grabbed Humberto's hand. Not smooth but not the rough hands of a laborer.

# 22

Driving east on I-10, there is still no word from Humberto and Tomas continued to get angrier. Pedro had text them as he traveled close enough to shore for signal strength. After sending the "all's well", he traveled further south before more east.

Tomas is thinking that he must assume that Humberto is out. "If he is still alive, I will end that too." he said under his breath.

Tomas driving thought about all he had to do as Jose slept in the front passenger's seat. Each member carried a phone with strict instructions to call only Tomas. They do not know each other's phone information. Tomas carried a SIM's card bundle with him in the event he needs to change his number. If that happened, Tomas would notify his controllers overseas of the new number change via email. They would send the new contact information to the others and direct them to change their SIM if needed. The others only backup was to send a message via WhatsApp to a controller in Mexico for instructions.

The drive was long and uneventful stopping only for gas and food. Tomas made sure they always cleaned their vehicle to not have the appearance of traveling far. If stopped by the police, he knew these were things they looked for with drug smugglers. He did not want to waste time. They continued east until turning south on Interstate 75 in Florida. The plan is inching together. The target is getting closer. Anticipation increased as he read the mileage marker, "Tampa 267 miles".

Pedro continued across the Gulf without incident. He expects no problems this far out. As you get closer to state waters, there is a chance of encountering a marine patrol unit. Only the Coast Guard patrols these waters and they don't care about a lone shrimp boat enroute to Florida from Texas. The common alien and smuggling routes are further south. It will be a week before the *Mary Beth* is reported overdue, maybe longer. He will be in Tampa by then. He charts his location and guesses at what point he will be close enough to Florida to receive cell service to send Tomas another message.

Three hours later, Tomas and Jose arrive in the city limits of Tampa. They have directions to the downtown Greyhound Bus station. Tomas removes the key given him from the package Jose received at the hotel. He looks at Jose and says, "Wait here, I'll be back."

Jose got out and leaned against the car to stretch. Tomas walks inside and found a small bank of lockers. He inserts the key and opens locker 127. Inside is a sports bag weighing about 10 pounds. He turns and walks out without looking inside and places it into the back of the van. They drive east to Brandon, a suburb of Tampa with a large population and equal traffic. Florida is similar to Texas with its large Hispanic population. They will fit in well. They check into a Fairfield Inn off Highway 60 and I-75.

In their room Jose asked, "What's in the bag and what do we do now?"

Tomas did not say anything, placing the bag on his bed and opening it. He looks inside and removes several one-pound packs of C4 explosives.

Tomas looks at Jose and said, "The start."

He smiled and laid on the bed to await word from Pedro.

"For now, my friend we rest. There is much work ahead and rest is valuable."

It will be another 18 hours before receiving another text from Pedro that said, "2 away and all is great."

Tomas responded, "At home."

He sent the same message to a memorized number he was told to text when settled. To this one, he includes their address.

# 23

"What does this mean Humberto?" pointing to the symbol in the new bible.

"Where am I? Who are you? I don't understand what you are doing?"

"I asked you a question Bert!"

"Fuck you. I…"

Before he could say another word, Peter hit him in the stomach. The blow took him off guard as he struggles to get air into his lungs. Peter uses this tactical move because Humberto is unprepared and it will knock the breath out of him and leave no bruising.

"I'll ask you again, Bert, what is this drawing in the bible?"

Humberto looked at him only this time with anger. His eyes tighter and he clinched his jaw. With most aliens seeking a better life, they have been raised poor and in an authoritarian state. They know never to raise an angry emotion in the face of authority. The results are brutal. There was another knock on the door and Sarah looked in.

"I want an attorney!" He yelled to ensure Sarah and whoever was outside the door can hear. Sarah ignored him.

"There it is you piece of shit! You are not Mexican. You're Venezuelan and what are you and the others doing here?"

"Peter, our analyst recognizes what the symbol is." Sarah said.

Peter looked at Humberto and back at Rafael, who again got in his face and berating him in Spanish.

In the living room Peter asked, "What do you have?"

"Pat brought this to my attention. This symbol is an old cipher technique." Peter's mind is turning with the information.

"What do you mean old? Can we break it?"

"We can if we had the key. This is a pigpen code and has been around for centuries. It is simplistic and with all our technologies today, we have forgotten much of the old stuff. Lucky for us, Pat is a student of old games and codes. She recognized the XO gaming style. The way it works is you take any geometric shape and insert symbols or even letters within that shape that match the alphabet. With a key, you can decipher it. Without it, well, impossible. Pat's looking into computer algorithms to help."

"This is a confirmation that Humberto, or whatever his name is, is wrong. They are dirty, and I think there is something worse planned."

"One more thing. The FBI has a group brought in by the Border Patrol from the same area as Humberto. They may have been together as we talked about earlier."

He went into the room and nodded to Rafael to follow him. Outside he told him, "The FBI has brought up seven people they think could have been part of a larger group of aliens arrested a mile from Humberto. Let's confirm our idea. Take Bert's picture and go talk to them. Gather more information and call me if anything good comes out of it."

Rafael took the picture and left. Peter walked back in the room.

"Ok Bert let's start again. What is your real name?"

"Humberto Santos, I told you that a hundred times already. I also told you that I want an attorney. You cannot question me anymore until I have an attorney. Your laws protect me from people like you."

"Ok Bert. Your situation is an emergency and people's lives are at stake. You lost your rights when you and your friends crossed over to do harm to America. Listen Bert, get used to it. You belong to me until I am satisfied with your answers. No one knows where you are and there is no one coming to help. It is you against us and we will win, one way or another. All I need is a little info from someone else about you and things are going to change. This will become very bad for you. We will be here for as long as it takes, or you can take. One way or the other, if you ever want to do something for yourself, now is the time to do it. I do not believe you had anything to do with the death of those agents, but you know who did. We are already breaking your bible code and if you make us do all the work, there is no way we can help you. Now is the time to do the right thing for yourself. I know how these things work. You are young and everyone uses you. You have to do as told. You get no respect. I know how important respect is to a man. Now is your time to climb to the top."

Peter will use a series of themes to see which one has an effect. Each angle will be tried and if there is no response, he will switch. He knew how the different generations responded to pressure and what strikes a nerve. Young people believe they are entitled without earning. This is especially true in Latin cultures where boys believe they are men and men are in charge. Working on his ego and pride is creating a positive response. Humberto has stopped interrupting and is listening to what was said.

# 24

Tomas and Jose lounged around the hotel room. There is no way they are going to leave the room with the explosives. They could not imagine the disgrace if this entire operation fell apart because of a nosy cleaning lady. Room service or take out only, as long as one person stayed. Since Tomas was charged with the responsibility of the operation, that person was him. Whenever there is a need for towels and such, one of them would step out and meet the maids and switch towels and get fresh soap.

Pedro arrived in Tampa and docked at the Tampa Shrimp docks on Causeway Boulevard. He decides not to call Tomas, yet. He learned never trust anyone in this business too fast.

"Just look at Sani and Kurt." He said to himself aloud. "They trusted, and they are gone."

He waited a few hours and watched the activity on the docks. The shrimping community is a rough group who trust no one, especially anyone outside of the business. Between competition, marine enforcement officers, and environmental regulators, it is hard enough to survive.

Tomas received a text message that read, "Meet woman in white Toyota in the parking lot. She will say 'pana', reply 'ricarda.' She will give you a package."

Like others in this business, you can never trust a criminal. Tomas walked into the parking lot and saw a white Toyota parked nearby in a space and he approached. The front passengers window opened, and he saw a female in the driver's seat. She smiled and said, "Hola pana."

Tomas replied with, "Ricarda."

She had seen his photo before the meeting that was set up to confirm his identity. It gave them the opportunity to observe Tomas in case something had gone wrong and thus protecting the main people. Tomas was given a piece of notebook paper that read, "Food court, Brandon mall."

She placed the car into reverse and drove away. As Tomas re-entered the hotel he stopped inside and watched through the plate glass. A Chevy SUV in the rear of the parking lot pulled out behind the Toyota even though he never saw anyone get into the SUV. This told him they had been inside throughout. "Theirs or ours?" He thought to himself. He will remember the description. After returning to the room, he saw Jose looking out the window.

"Did you see everything?"

"Only what was visible from here, no faces and such."

"Did you notice the Chevy?"

"Yes, the one that left after the Toyota, but again no one inside. The windows were tinted too dark. What did they say?"

"Find out what you can about the Brandon mall food court and include all exits. I need you to conduct counter-surveillance. We will take our package with us. We leave in 5 minutes."

He felt alarmed because he still had not heard from Pedro since Texas and nothing from Humberto. Without them, this operation is in jeopardy, a thought he could not accept. The Brandon mall was close.

"Go outside and walk through the parking lot, but do not make it too obvious what you are doing. Call my phone and talk about what you see. I will get ready with the speaker on. I will hear you if something is wrong. Make sure there are no other cars with people in them."

Jose said nothing as he left the room. Tomas went to the window and watched as Jose walked around the parking lot talking on the phone.

With no one else around, Tomas told Jose to start and wait in the van and he will meet him there. Tomas went downstairs carrying the backpack. They drove the mile to the mall in 10 minutes due to the traffic and parked on the west side. They entered near Dick's Sporting Goods and walked to the opposite side of the mall to the food court. The noise with all the people was deafening. He knew this was a good spot for the meet and told Jose to choose a different table where he could see him. Now he waited.

A moment later, his phone went off. The text read, "Be there soon."

"Nicely timed text." He thought to himself. They must have eyes on him already. The fact that they asked him no identifying questions said that they already knew what he looked like. This made him more uncomfortable considering he had not heard from the others.

Pedro finished tying off at the guest dock. He filled the tanks as he looked over the area. A man approached wearing calf high white rubber boots and called out, "Hey, you the Captain?"

Pedro grinning with his familiar ear to ear grin yelled back, "Yes, I am. I'm the only one aboard. Doin some maintenance before looking for another crew for a couple of weeks. Going down to the Keys."

He knew by offering the possibility for work, no one would object if he stayed there for a few days.

"Sure, no problem, Captain, log in at the front. Over there." He said pointing to the blue colored aluminum building on the end.

"If you intend to be here more than a day, they'll have to charge you a fee for dock usage, power, water and such."

"No problem. Will do. Maybe here a week or two at most. Thanks."

Pedro knew there would be no prying into anything here for a while and after an hour, he decided to text Tomas.

Tomas had been sitting at the table for half an hour and knew they too were conducting counter-surveillance on the area. If they knew him, they would know Jose as well. However, he kept the situation the same. Jose can oversee the area around him during the meeting. He watched as Hispanic men walked by expecting any one of them to be his contact. People came and went, arms filled with shopping bags. Two women sat at the table next to him and placed their department store bags on the ground next to them. They began eating their Chinese food from containers and having a conversation. He could not help noticing the one in a dress. It was yellow and cut to mid-thigh when she sat and crossed her legs. She was young in her mid-twenties with long blonde hair. She had an athletic build; thin and muscular. You did not see women like this in his barrio. He continued to look around and glanced at his watch. Another 10 minutes passed when the woman's phone next to her rang. She said nothing and then leaned over towards him.

"Pardon me, sir."

Tomas' heart picked up a beat.

He looked at her and smiled, "Yes?"

"Tell Jose to stay where he is. How was your trip?"

# 25

Peter continued taking calculating angles with Humberto to see if one connected. He has been tied to the chair for 14 hours. Humberto was arrested a day and a half ago and Peter knew time was of the essence. This is the only window into the case. Nothing was working and he knew he had to change direction again. He believes Humberto is his real name.

"Bert. You must be at the bottom of the operational chain to be using your real name." There it was! He saw the twitch in the left eye and knew to stay on this course of interviewing.

"Not only did you have to use your real name, they made you cross with a group of aliens. Did you enjoy that, Bert?"

Seven of the others in the group were caught by CBP. Rafael went over to interview them in Spanish with a photograph of Humberto Santos. A woman in the group identified his picture. She had not wanted to talk, but when she was told that Humberto was a child molester and trying to run a child prostitution ring in both countries, she agreed to tell. Rafael called Peter about the positive identification and explain how the coyote lied about the Border Patrol making everyone panic.

"Well Bert," he continued to annoy him with the nickname, "the coyote kid who brought you here is still laughing at how fast all you 'pollo's' ran."

Humberto smiled and said, "I doubt that."

Peter was surprised by this one admission and the joy it gave Humberto. He knew it was important and made a mental note of it. Peter completed his questions and moved out the door and approached Sarah.

"Have Rafi talk to the others about the coyote and ask the Mexican authorities to look over the area south of the crossing. Running on a hunch."

A good interviewer knows when and where during the process to take a personal break. It allows him the opportunity to confer with others watching from outside the room on CCTV and get more information for the next round of the interview. Rafael returned and told Peter during one of these breaks that the coyote's body was found.

Peter continued to interview him, "You should know that I do not think you are as low as they believe you are. You were smart enough to slip away from the others when tricked in believing the Border Patrol was nearby or were you."

Humberto looked at him.

"Tricked I mean. Were you set up or was it fate? There are reasons why we caught you so fast. Others are slipping information."

Peter let the mind virus sink in as he watched for a reaction.

Humberto looked down and to the left. He was thinking about what Peter had said. He is having an internal dialogue with himself. Peter sees it's an emotional topic, so he does not interrupt. He allows the psychological virus to spread.

After a moment Peter asks in a low voice, "Did the others see you as different from them? Is that why you became their scapegoat?"

Humberto shifted in his chair and did not look at Peter. Peter knew he was on the right track. There were others and Humberto believes the others may have used him to get through.

With the theory in place, Peter pushes it further without telling him anything.

"I know you received the necessary training and that we have you because any other way except information, you wouldn't be here."

Peter is choosing his words carefully avoiding negation words like "not". Many investigators will ask this same question with negations such as, "You would not be here had you not done well." The negations of "not" highlight an all-negative question making it easier for Humberto to say "no".

He continued. "Why do the others think different about you? Now is your chance. Your only chance that I can provide to do something different for yourself. Something better. Be appreciated for what you can accomplish."

Peter is being positive as he recognizes Humberto is listening.

"Accomplish! What do you mean? I have been arrested."

Now is the time for Peter to start into positive reinforcements and choice.

"I mean you can do the right thing and I can help you. I can move you and your family. I can have papers drafted to help bring you and your family to America. Give them all a chance. I have been with you long enough to see that you are not a bad person. Sometimes, good people get involved with bad things because it is out of their control. It can be societal or peer pressures that often drive good men to do bad things."

He paused a moment and said, "There is option two. Turn you over to the Mexican cartel family related to the dead teen found south of the border where you crossed. He must have pissed you off to get you to go back over the border."

Peter see's the shock in Humberto's expression. He is thinking, "How can they know so much?"

The others in the group said they were across the border when they were abandoned. Peter knew something happened to force Humberto to go south again and then return.

"There is no one else." Humberto replied. "What others? It was not me. I never have hurt anyone."

Peter could see the growing surprise and concerns on his face.

"They are not as nice as we are. With us there is a chance. No chances exist with them. They do not like their people murdered."

All was quiet for a moment and then Peter said, "There are always others who are quick to talk for gain."

There it was. Another mind virus.

"Gain? What gain?"

"Humberto," Peter uses his real name to give him back a little dignity. "It is the topic of gain which is universal to all. Money and security."

Humberto sat and thought about it a moment and then said. "I can see some who would be interested, but others who would never be."

Playing on the information he was leaking that there are members of the group who are not so fanatical as to understand the meaning of money, but he did not mention security.

Peter looked at him and said, "That is why I am talking to you Humberto. Some were interested, but not all. If you know anything about America, it is that we have a lot of money. That's why it's called "the land of dreams" for people around the world. We are willing to pay to keep it that way. To keep it safe. There are things that can be done for you and I am the only person who can do it. All I need from you is help. Tell me what you know. Let's stop what is happening before it is too late."

"If you know so much already, why do you need me?"

This confirms to Peter something is happening. He continues, "Because like you said, not everyone is willing to play along, but some are."

Taking a calculated risk, he then added, "They knew enough about you and where you were. However, they said that they do not know all the details."

"That's because only Tomas knows the most."

"Tomas?" Peter asked.

"Si, Tomas Guerra. At home we know him as Fauzi."

"Home?"

"Venezuela."

"Thanks Humberto, there are things in life that are worth the risk. Your information is but the operation is not. Let's talk."

Peter knows to be empathetic when the interviewee provides information and why Humberto was the low man on the proverbial totem pole.

# 26

Tomas is thinking to himself, "What kind of bull shit is this. This is his contact? A Hispanic male following Islamic rules to take directions from a woman!"

The woman turns towards him and says with a smile on her face, "I see you found the package you needed at the bus station. I have to ask you, is it such a smart idea to bring it into here?"

Tomas knew her accent was not Spanish. It was Persian. As in all languages, each has its own dialect. Everyone with that language as their first recognizes where others are from. From his years around them, he knew it was Iranian.

Jose sitting nearby sees Tomas start talking to these women.

"What the hell is he doing. Now is not the time for this."

He stood to approach as Tomas and the woman both looked at him with anger and he stopped. Tomas shook his head in the negative and directed him to sit back down. She was beautiful, but there was something dangerous in the way she changed expressions and looked at him that scared him even more than Tomas. He sat back down.

Tomas was running the ideas through his head and decided it was best to tell her the truth. His phone went off. He looked at the text message from Pedro. "I am at the docks in Tampa on Causeway Boulevard near Port Tampa."

Tomas felt relieved to have received the text. He had dreaded telling whoever was in charge that he has not heard from half of his crew. One was a sustainable loss.

"I had no choice in the matter today. There is the two of us and the boat is having maintenance. I have not heard from one."

She sat there a moment and said, "Humberto?"

"Yes, not a word. The last time was in Mexico waiting to cross. There was a delay."

"The delay, yes, I read about the delay. I will assume there were no other delays. It is reported as drug border violence." She pauses a moment and then says, "I am told Humberto is the least of your operatives."

Tomas feeling better says, "Yes, we can continue without him."

He is thinking that she is well informed. He knows she is or connected to someone who is high in command.

"I have something for you. It is in a mailbox in Riverview, a small community south of here. This is the key for a box at the UPS store. You will find more information there for your mission. This is a number to an associate who will send any information. On the other side is a Gmail account. We can communicate in the drafts section as you were shown. We should not have a need to talk again."

She laughs and stands along with the other woman. She never glances at Jose and walks towards the glass doors leading outside. Tomas watches for a moment. He sees no one else. He stands and Jose follows. They met in the mall and took their time looking through the store fronts. They walked as planned into an employee hallway that exits to the outside in a nonpublic lot. It is an easy way to lose a tail if you are followed and they walk to the van and drive back to the hotel.

"What happened? Who was that? Was that our contact?" Jose asked.

"She has given us our plans. She is a messenger for the boss. Pedro has contacted me. This is where he is. Drop me off at the hotel and go get him. Then I want you to go to this location in Riverview. One of you stay outside and the other go inside to this mailbox."

He hands Jose the key he was given.

"Do not open anything. Understood!"

Jose nodded.

"Bring it all back to the room. We have planning to consider."

"Do you know what the target is?" Jose asked.

"Bring it to me."

"What about Humberto, have you heard anything? Can we complete our task without him, or will they replace him?"

Tomas looks at him a moment and says "Do not concern yourself with my responsibilities. I will let you know when and how it will happen and with who, when you need to know. Pay attention and drive."

At the hotel, Tomas removes his SIM card and setup reactivation of his phone. Later he will notify Jose and Pedro of the new number.

# 27

Peter places a call to John Hatfield in Miami with the updated information told by Humberto. He is using a secure satellite phone, a Globalstar CDMA signal phone operating with a system of satellites. The technology converts speech into digital from the ground to the satellite and back to the receiver. Every call has its own unique code and is impossible to cut into without the code, which again changes at the next call.

"Things are coming together." Peter said.

"Good. I don't want to hold you up. Do we know what's going on yet?"

"Not yet, but we will. I need you to use every avenue to collect information on a Tomas or Fauzi Guerra. We have started on this end as well."

"Is this our guy?"

"He may be the one who killed the agents. There are more of them as suspected, but we don't know for sure how many or their plan. They are here for something from Venezuela. Our guy is starting to open up. I will know more soon."

"Your guesswork earlier is sounding dead on."

"Sounding more like it. Any luck on the video surveillance from the areas after the murders?"

"Nothing we can go on. Listen Peter, the FBI is doing back flips out here. No worries though. I am keeping our upper levels informed and they are pleased with the progress. As long as we continue forward, there will be no problems from the outside."

"Roger that. I'll call you." Peter finished the call and understood the "need to produce" message he was given.

He got a Coke and returned to the room. Humberto sat there feeling a little dejected.

"You alright?"

"How would you feel?"

"Listen Humberto, lets ease up a little. I'll cut you out of the chair. No problems, right?"

"Yes please. No problemos."

Peter cut off the tape that had him bound to the chair. Slow to bring his arms forward his shoulders were stiff as he rubbed his wrist and said, "You said you can help me. Now is the time and I will consider telling all I know."

Peter started to get angry but controlled himself to explain the rules. "I can help you, but you will have to understand a few things. I call the shots. You do whatever I ask and if I catch you in one lie, the whole deal is off. Do you understand?"

Humberto agreed.

"Good. This has nothing to do with your considerations. Only my considerations matter. For now, at least until you prove you are willing to play."

This demonstrates his authority over him but shows his willingness to allow Humberto to prove himself.

From the next room, Sarah calls out, "Peter come here."

Peter walked out the door. He knew he could not trust Humberto and left his feet tied. Once a bad guy, always a bad guy. He's mad at the others because he was not given as much respect as he thought he deserved. But at the same time, given a chance, he would cut our throat in a second as he had the "coyote".

Peter walked in the room, "What's up?"

"This came in. Meet Fauzi Guerra. CIA had this as part of their investigations of collusion between Iran and the Venezuelan government. He is an up and comer with many operations under his belt for the Chavez regime and now the new dictator."

In his hand he was holding a blurred black and white photograph. He stared at the face that was looking to the left of the photographer who must have been across the street while sitting at a cafe. The area is South America. Probably Venezuela with what we know.

"Let's test ole Burt." Peter said as he returned into the room.

Humberto was looking at him and what he was holding. Peter walks straight to him and hands him the photograph.

"Who is this, Humberto?" He saw the reaction in his face.

"Well señor, it is an older…"

"Remember what I said Humberto. Just one fucking lie and we are done here. I am not going to keep reminding you. You will have to survive or not with your own choices. But I will know."

Peter wants to remove opportunities for Humberto to test whether anything will happen if he lies.

Humberto sat for a second and said, "That's him."

"That's who?"

"That is an older picture, but that is Tomas."

"Where is Tomas."

"I was supposed to contact him, I am certain he thinks I have failed them. This is why I was sent through in such a way."

Continuing to play on him and deepen the mind virus Peter said, "Maybe he sent you the way he did and with the information we had, they wanted you caught. You were the expendable pawn in the plot. You would be the distraction. Two Border Patrol Agents are murdered using the exact type of weapons you were carrying near the same time and area you are crossing. Arrest you for the murders and you will get the death penalty while they get away. Resist and you would have died. Not carry out your mission, they would kill you. Now that we are on to their game against you, stay with me. Work with me. I will help you. You have to tell the truth. We can get through many things together, but we cannot get past a lie. Do you understand?"

Peter is making use of words focusing on those that demonstrate a team such as "we".

Humberto sat there a moment thinking.

"Are you with me partner." Peter says still playing into his narcissistic mind by using the word "partner" to mean an equal, something he has not had.

Humberto smiled and nodded his head and said, "The destination is Tampa in Florida. This is all I know. I was to contact them."

"How were you to contact them?"

"I should have text them."

"Can you still?"

"This much time gone by, I do not know if they would believe me. I am still a couple of days away."

"I need his number and I will have you there tonight. Then you can contact him from a phone. Tell him about the delay and the chase in the desert and lost equipment."

"I can try, si, I can try. I do not have my phone anymore. How do I explain how I traveled across the country?"

"How were you supposed to travel?"

"I was to buy an old car once I got here."

Peter has recognized his use of "them" but he has to complete the communication issues first to stay on topic. He is talking and now is not the time for confusions. One subject at a time.

"We will get you one and a phone. How many are there? You keep saying "them".

"I trained with two. There is a fourth, an old man has been gone or here for a long time."

"What do you mean gone?"

"He has been in the US for a while. I saw him early in the training and then no more. I overheard it said that he would be somewhere waiting."

"Do you know where?"

"No."

"What are their names?"

"I only know them as Tomas, Jose, and Pedro. Pedro is the one already here. I was kept out of most information so that is all I know."

"What else can you tell us about them?" Sarah asked.

"Jose is a close associate of Tomas and the reason I get left out."

"Last names?" Peter asked.

"I don't know."

"Ok. Listen to me carefully. What are you all going to do in Tampa?"

"I do not know. Tomas is to receive the orders when we arrive."

"From who?"

"I do not know."

"You said a moment ago that you trained with others. Trained for what and by who? Is this for drugs, intelligence or what? You must know the type of operation."

"Yes. It will be an attack on something. We were all trained by Iranians."

Sarah looked at Peter and said, "Not much to go on. I'll start on the phone number."

"Thanks. More than we had." Peter thought a second and repeated, "A hell of a lot more than we had. Let's get to Tampa."

# 28

Zarrin was raised in Iran. Her father, Ostad Kaled Hosseini, was a respected weapons developer for the Ayatollah. Ostad is an honorific name given him for his actions when he lost his left arm in the battle that killed a disloyal cleric. Zarrin is the youngest daughter of Ostad. As a woman in the male dominated Muslim culture, Zarrin never accepted her subservient role. Her father respected her spirit and raised her as the son he lost in the war with Iraq. He used his position to give her the influence she wanted and had her trained in special weapons and tactics while clearing the path for her to rise to a position of power. It is not unusual to find women in combat roles in the Iranian army. They are often in the secret police or disposable front-line troops. Zarrin was trained to organize and lead activities for Iranian interest.

Zarrin Banu means "golden lady". She had proved herself many times and brought honor to her family's name. She was promoted to direct certain activities of the Republican Guard, Iran's elite troops after assassinating an Iraqi ambassador she lured to his room at a French hotel and drugged him. French authorities determined he had died of a heart attack. The Iraqi's were always suspicious.

She requested and was given important duties in South America. It is an area others do not want to go but she knew it was where she could excel. Instructing others is a talent where she surpasses most. Training is essential because they are on the back door of the great Satan itself, America. Overseeing the training of FARC rebels with success, she was given an added role of assisting in a plan to strike at the United States. She leaped at the opportunity and was given wide latitude to train personnel and allowed to choose half of the teams herself.

Though they had never seen her, she chose, Fauzi Guerra and Pedro Gomez based on their experience. Fauzi had insisted on the help of Jose Arriba and the local garrison commander, Francisco Alvarez could draft in one of his own. He chose his nephew Humberto Santos. Humberto was always the outcast and a problem child. His heart was elsewhere, but he wanted to please his uncle. Time with the others soon showed him his place in the group.

Zarrin had planned with members of the Iranian military with the approval of the Iranian prime minister the plan to change the wars in the Middle East. She explained that to hurt the beast, you had to cut off its head. She is in Tampa to oversee the plan. She is the most dangerous woman Tomas has ever met, he just did not know it, yet.

Zarrin Banu walked out to her BMW with her assistant Parvin after the meeting. She often will ask for opinions from her subordinates, a habit viewed by many in her culture as a weakness. Parvin has been a loyal friend and protector of the Banu family for as long as she could remember. Zarrin trusts her over all others.

"What do you think of them?" She asked.

"He seems like a capable man. He appears determined and strong. Is that not the reason you chose him?"

She nodded her head as they drove out of the parking lot. She had sought a confirmation of the traits she had seen in him as well.

"We will see."

# 29

Six hours later, Peter and his team are landing at Tampa Executive Airport, a small private airport outside Tampa International. Sarah found out during the flight that the number she has for Tomas is no longer in service. They found two dropped off rental cars and an old car with temporary paper plates from Arizona, sent by John Hatfield. Peter drives Humberto while Sarah and Rafael drive the rentals to Plant City, a small agricultural town east of Tampa and stop at a hotel next to Interstate 4. They wanted a location, away from the main town, but close to a connecting Interstate for easy access in either direction.

Peter tells Humberto about the phone number and ask about the alternatives. Humberto explains how he has to go through the WhatsApp to get information and the call is made. He is told someone will be in touch with his number.

Waiting, Peter sees Humberto is nervous and says, "I know you're ready and everything is going to work. From what you have told me, they cannot be too far ahead in Tampa. Call Tomas."

"He will ask me why I waited until arriving in Tampa to call him. What will I say?"

"We have already covered this. Tell him the truth and lie. There were many problems at the border because of the deaths of the agents. You wanted to make sure you were here before contacting him to assure that all was clear."

Humberto receives the text on his prepaid throw away Boost phone the Team had picked up for him. Humberto is familiar with these phones and their use by anyone who does not want to be found. You buy no contract, get a number, throw it away when you have finished. It avoids GPS tracking of standard phones. What Humberto did not know was the tech guys in Tucson had loaded the phone with their own equipment. Every time the phone was used, the same information was passed to another phone that was with Rafael. He had the phone on vibrate and was in a separate room reading the same messages sent and received. Peter wanted Rafael on the phone for any language translations.

Tomas is sitting in the hotel room awaiting the return of Jose with Pedro when his phone signaled a text message in his WhatsApp forwarded from their controllers in Mexico. It included Humberto's new number.

He looked down and read, "Am near Tampa. Had many delays. Awaiting you."

Tomas was glad to hear from the final member of the team yet curious what had taken this long. He sat there a moment deciding his best course of action. He is a professional and does not trust coincidences.

"Why had he not contacted me before now?" he thought to himself looking at the different number. "I do not want direct contact yet."

Tomas pulled out a map of the area and looked at major roadways. He sees Fowler Avenue is north of Brandon and runs east-west from I75 to I275. He recognizes that there are large entertainment centers, a university, and a mall. This area will be busy. He then looks up restaurants along the road and finds what he wants.

He returns the message to forward his response and says, "Meet me at the Perkins restaurant on Fowler Avenue and 50th Street in three hours."

He awaits the return of the others with the package. When they arrive, he informs them of Humberto and the plans as they drive out to meet him.

Humberto looked at Peter who said, "Show me."

He read the message from the phone. It was in Spanish and he did see Perkins, 3 horas, and Fowler Avenue. Rafael entered the room as Humberto said pacing, "Will he trust me? I do not know if I can do this. He is not speaking directly to me. He does not trust me."

"Listen, we have been through this a hundred times. It makes sense that he is being cautious. You are late contacting him. You will do fine. You have practiced your story to the point it sounds natural. Let's get this done. Answer him."

He sent a confirmation text, "Ok."

Peter then looked at Rafael and Sarah and before he can say anything Sarah looks up from her phone and says, "I've got the address and texted it to each of you. We're 45 minutes away with traffic."

Peter said, "Thanks. Let's go now and scout the area. I'll drive with Humberto. Keep the surveillance loose. I am certain the time delay is for the same reason on their end."

"Will do." Rafael said as he looked at Sarah. They gathered their bags and left.

Peter looked at Humberto and asked, "Is there anything specific you are supposed to say, ask, or lead off with as a signal?"

"No nothing. We all know each other."

"There has to be a catch phrase to use in case of danger?"

"No, there was nothing I was told."

Peter thought this sounds strange. He had never heard of any type of operation that did not have a danger or abort signal.

"Remember what we talked about." Peter said.

"Si, I know. I am not going to double cross you."

Peter and Humberto left the room and entered the old car. They drove past the Perkins address once they arrived to the area. He called Sarah who said she was on the University of South Florida campus across the street from the restaurant and they met near the SunDome sports arena.

As they pulled up to Sarah's car, Peter walked over and told Humberto to stay in the car to avoid any possibility of detection.

"Where's Rafael?" Peter asked.

"He's at the Museum of Science and Industry across the street. There are two entrances, one facing Fowler Avenue on the south side of the restaurant and the other on 50th Street facing west. Rafael will cover the Fowler Avenue door and I will cover the 50th Street entrance. The parking lot is in the front, the side on 50th Street and in the back. There is an apartment complex behind the restaurant."

"Ok. If this goes as I suspect, this will not be the meeting place. They will change it several times until they are comfortable."

Sarah understood and nodded.

Peter walked back to Humberto.

"Listen to me. There is nothing to worry about. Focus on what you're doing with confidence, practice some deep breathing and you won't look nervous."

"Will I be wearing any type of wire?"

"No, I thought about it and decided you shouldn't until we know they trust you. The difference is we always trust partners."

Peter is still playing on his emotions. "Let's go over everything again. They will be suspicious for waiting so long to contact them. It is good that you are local and can explain time delays. As practiced, let them know that two border patrol agents were killed, and they increased enforcement all along the border. This made it harder for anyone to cross. Act as if you don't know what happened in the desert. All the information has not been released. Describe every moment that happened from the crossing to the chase and your escape. Let them know how you went in a different direction from the others when your coyote left you all. This way you only have to lie about being caught and not the other information. You have reviewed the maps and the car lot location where your vehicle was purchased along with a description of the salesman, where you stopped to eat along the way, and we put some cash receipts for gas and food at spots on the route to give you proof."

The team had re-created the car purchase and trip to coach Humberto on the flight over. They knew Tomas and the others could ask him questions he had to be prepared to answer. Humberto nodded and looked down. It was obvious he was going through events in his mind. He was afraid of Tomas. This is a tense moment for all involved.

Realizing this Peter says, "Don't worry Humberto, it will be fine. You are as good as anyone here or there." Still playing on his confidence levels.

Peter's phone rang, it was Rafael.

"Peter, all is quiet. Little traffic in and out."

"Ok, were gonna send him over in a minute."

"Roger that."

"You ready?" Peter said to Humberto.

"Ready. I am ready. Muchos gracias señor for the help. I will not let you down."

"I know. Partners never let each other down." Peter replied and smiled.

Sarah smiled at him as he drove out. She looked at Peter and said, "What do you think. Is he legit or bullshit?"

"We are about to find out. Are you ready?"

"Yep, when you get back, we'll listen." She replied.

They had left out several pieces of information. The phone carried by Humberto was also wired as a listening device. Any and all communications, either by phone or conversation could be followed. His car was rigged with a kill switch. This is a device connected to the engine and controlled by remote in the event he reconsidered, they could flip a switch and turn off the engine. The plan is in motion.

# 30

Humberto drives north of Fowler Avenue to Fletcher Avenue and turns west. He turns south on 56th Street and then west on Fowler to look like he was arriving at the restaurant. He parked behind it as instructed. Peter followed with the kill switch in case he changed his mind. He drove past the restaurant, turned north on 50th Street and right again into the apartment complex next to Sarah.

After 10 minutes, Humberto's phone rang. It was Tomas.

"Are you there?"

"Yes, I am."

"We are running a little late. Drive west on Fowler Avenue and go a few miles and you will see a mall on the right. Meet us there. Behind the tire shop in the parking lot on the east end." The phone hung up before he could say anything.

Rafael radioed, "Peter, they called him and moved the meet to the mall behind the tire shop. They called soon after he arrived so they may have eyes on as well. They used a regular phone. I sent the number to Sarah."

"I knew this was going to happen."

Rafael walked across the parking lot and got in his car. He was in a controlled hurry mode. If there is counter-surveillance they will be watching for anyone out of the ordinary.

Peter got out of his car and into Sarah's and said, "I'll leave my car here and ride with you to cut down on the number of vehicles in case of any surveillance. We have a phone number they called from. I'll need you to follow up on it when we are done here."

"Yeah, I got it from Rafi. If you can call it in while I drive it we will be ahead of the game."

Sarah and Peter drive out to watch Humberto as the number is relayed back to the office. Humberto pulls out and drives west. They see him turn and keep him in sight. Rafael drives out from the rear parking lot of the museum and turns into the heavy traffic. Humberto drives in the right lane watching for the mall.

Jose is driving the van with Tomas in the right front seat and Pedro in the back. Tomas has already pulled the SIM and battery out of his phone. He will replace it with a new one later and a new number. Jose can call Humberto if needed. They watched from a gas station as Humberto drove from the restaurant. They are a couple of car lengths back in the center lane.

"Did either of you see anyone?" Tomas asked.

"No." They both responded at the same time.

"I do not like it. I do not trust him."

"It all seems to check out." Jose said. "He has the car with Arizona plates."

"Why has he not called in before now?" Tomas said.

Pedro said nothing, but knew Tomas was thinking the same as he about not trusting unusual delays.

"Pedro, you ready?" Tomas asked.

"Si."

"I'm not taking any chances. Let's do it now."

Tomas looked at Jose and said, "Pull alongside of him."

Pedro opened the side door to the van as Jose sped up. They pull up to the side of Humberto's car as he looks ahead and to the right for the mall. Pedro lines up the sights of his pistol and fires. The bullet shatters the driver's side window and strikes Humberto in the left temple. A small hole appears and blood splatters across the front of his dash and windshield from the exit hole in his head. His body falls to the right supported by the seatbelt.

Peter and Sarah are driving west watching Humberto's car moving slow in the right lane. Suddenly, his car turns to the right, travels off the road, through a ditch and crashes against a tree.

"What the hell?" Peter says.

Other drivers stop and some run over to the car. Others slow down and then continue. Peter knows to watch the reactions of other drivers, not the crash. If this is the result of one of the other drivers, they will act unlike others. He sees a minivan never slow and continue straight.

"Do you see the van up ahead, the maroon one?" Peter asked while pointing.

"Yeah. Wanna follow it?"

"Get up there as fast as you can."

Peter calls Rafael. "Rafi, Humberto's car crashed. Stop and see what happened. Try to pull our kill switch from the engine. We're going to check out a maroon van."

The van went straight through the next intersection and made a left at 22$^{nd}$ street. Sarah drives up to the intersection and runs the red light. She speeds down the road to catch the van but doesn't see it.

"Where did they go?" Peter said.

"Must have turned behind us."

Jose made a left after clearing the intersection and rushed into the parking lot of an apartment complex. They watch as a silver car driven by a woman with a man in the right front seat runs the red light and speeds past. They drive out and turn north to Fowler Avenue from where they had come.

Tomas speaking to himself out loud said, "And who are you?"

Jose said, "Maybe they're the police?"

Pedro speaks up, "No, the police would have lights and sirens."

Tomas knew he was right not to trust Humberto and said, "Let's get back to the hotel. We must speed up our plans. Do not drive past the scene. It is a common mistake."

They turned west at Fowler Avenue in the opposite direction of the crash.

Peter's phone rang, and he saw it was Rafael, "Go ahead."

"Listen Peter, he's been shot once in the left temple. The shooter must have been in an adjacent car. It is not a rifle hit. He's dead. I pulled the switch out under the ruse of making sure there was no fire created by cutting the battery cables."

Peter did not say anything for a second and then told Rafael to scan the area for a maroon minivan, plates unknown. Rafael was stuck in the traffic, but he knew that bad guys like to return to the scene of the crime to see all the action. He parks in the median and after an hour, left.

Peter called John in Miami and let him know what happened.

"God Dammit!" John yells into the phone. "At least tell me we have some actionable intel to use!"

After a brief hesitation Peter says, "They are driving a maroon minivan. We talked about it on this end and I think we should call the van description to the local authorities. If something bad happens and it is discovered we had intel and kept it to ourselves, people will be pissed. We also have the number he called from and Sarah is looking into that now."

John thought about it and said, "You're right. Go ahead and make the calls."

After hanging up, Peter had Sarah stop on the side of the road. He put on a baseball hat and sunglasses and walks to a payphone and calls 911. He tells the operator that the killer of the man on Fowler Avenue is driving a maroon minivan. He hangs up and walks away. He knows the call will be traced to the location and the stores video surveillance cameras examined. The detectives are looking for any information from anyone about the identities of the shooter. They all return to the hotel in Plant City to work things out. Sarah informs all later that the number Tomas called from is no longer in service.

# 31

"Drop us off and get rid of the van and be sure no evidence can be found." Tomas tells Jose as they arrived at the hotel.

Jose knew what to do and drove to a gas station, bought a gas can, and filled it with two gallons. He drove to the entrance ramp of Interstate 75 southbound where he had noticed how this ramp ran parallel for miles with the interstate before splitting. Traffic in the left lane merges onto the interstate while traffic in the right lane exits to either north or south US301. He stops on the right shoulder between the first and second overpasses and gets out. The area is desolate and only passing traffic on the ramp can see him. He looks over the van for any items he may need and pours the gas into the interior. He removes the tag and opens the gas tank cap before checking again for traffic. Not seeing any, he tosses a lit cigarette through the window and moves away into the bushes. The van burst into flames and he stood and moves up the second overpass to a road and walks east where he can see the van engulfed in flames. He continues until he reaches a Wal-Mart parking lot, sees a white van, breaks into it, and drives off. These were skills taught to him as a young boy living in Caracas, not from the Iranians. He drives to the mall less than a mile away and throws the tag from the burnt van into a trash dumpster. He drove around the parking lot until he saw a van of the same color and make and swapped tags. The owner of the stolen van will report it to the police, and they will enter the tag in their computer database. If Jose's tag is ran by the police, it will come back to the correct make, color, and similar year. The other driver who had their tag swapped will never realize the plate was changed until they are stopped by the police for driving a suspected stolen van. It will not be until then that the real tag, that is on Jose's van, is entered into the system. This will take a while. Pleased with the outcome he returns to the hotel.

Tomas and Pedro sat at a table examining the contents of the package from the mailbox. Jose could tell there was excitement on their faces.

"Is everything alright?" Tomas said to him after closing the door.

"All is taken care of. I have replaced our vehicle and it is good."

Tomas nodded. He had confidence in his crew and glad Humberto is out of the picture. He did not pick or trust or like him.

Jose asked, "What about Humberto?"

Tomas replied, "It is obvious that he talked, but I made sure that he knew only what he had to know. I had feared such an event taking place and had overseen his orders. He knew little and besides; the first half of the plan is complete. Getting here. The second half of the operation can start. You will be, I can assure you, amazed."

Tomas and Pedro both smiled as Jose began to grin with anticipation for the news that has these two old time operatives so excited.

When Tomas opened the package, there were no detailed operations or orders. It named the target and the operation was his to determine. Jose came over to look and the others watched his eyes as his pupils dilated with excitement. The target location is MacDill Air Force base, home of Central Command. Multiple target ideas are his to make. They can attack one of the command centers. They can target personnel, gates, drive onto the base and create havoc to show the world Big Satan is vulnerable.

Jose looks up and says, "With just the three of us?"

"Let me worry about our numbers." Tomas said. "Besides, fewer has proven to be better in an operation this big. They will never prepare for such a small surgical strike even though they always depend on them for their own operations. Look at us as our countries Special Forces. They always strike hard and fast with few people."

Jose was smiling and nodding but thinking to himself what he can never tell the others, "All this is true except not like this. I see one old man, and the two of us."

Tomas said, "Tomorrow we will go out and begin our tactical surveillance. This needs to happen soon. There is still the problem caused by Humberto. We know they are looking for others in the area. The longer we are exposed the greater the chances of our failure."

They sat for a minute as Tomas thought. He lifted his head and looked at Pedro. "Take the boat out and scout the shoreline around the base. Find and mark all the boat ramps and check on security."

Pedro nodded.

"Jose, drive Pedro back to the boat and in the morning, watch the land gates to the base. See how people arrive and observe the security routines."

Jose knew not to ask questions. They had the latitude to respond as they thought best in these situations.

Speaking to Pedro he says, "Keep in contact and we will all meet again soon."

Tomas decided to get in touch with Zarrin Banu. He wanted to see if there could be others involved in the operation and to explain Humberto's security failures. Tomas sent a text message to Zarrin that read, "Do you want to meet for breakfast?"

Zarrin Banu was up late working on her laptop when her cell phone signaled a text message. She walked across the room and read the message. The instructions had always been to keep the plans simple to avoid the attention of the American government.

She texts back, "Tonight or tomorrow?"

"Tomorrow is fine but make it early before work."

"Ok, early. Good night."

# 32

Peter and the team returned to their hotel in Plant City. Gathering everyone he said, "What are they doing here? What are their plans? Why Tampa? I need each of us to produce a list of targets in the area. Do not restrict it to Tampa. Expand out 100 miles in any direction. Work on all the possibilities, but I know it is getting late. Let's break away from all this for a couple of hours and start fresh tomorrow."

He knew they were tired. They are running on little rest, which could cause a problem later. He also knew they had no idea what this group was doing and worse yet, their greatest chance rested on waiting for something to happen before they could move again. He hates being reactive instead of proactive.

The next morning at 5:00 AM, Zarrin advised Tomas to meet her at the Denny's on SR60 in Brandon. It is down the street from his hotel, and he arrives early. Anticipating her assistant Parvin, he got a table for three.

Moments later, they walk in and sit down. "What is going on my friend? You've changed numbers a few times." She asked.

Tomas said, "First of all I am down one person."

Zarrin did not say anything, but Tomas saw the micro expression of concern in her eyebrow.

He continued. "It's Humberto. He was working for the other team."

"How much has been lost?" she asked.

"There cannot be much. I did not know him and restricted how much he was given. He only knew to come here."

"He knew you, Jose, and Pedro did he not?"

"Only me and Jose. Pedro was already in Texas at the time. He may have seen or met him in the camps. He would not remember him if he had."

"Do we know about the other team?" she asked.

"All I know is maybe immigration or the local police."

"If this is related to the action on the border a few days back, then I would say it is the FBI. They are the investigating agency for such a crime."

"Maybe, but they do not know anything. Humberto has already been removed from the operation and we have reviewed the blueprint. The problem is in our numbers. Are there any more people to hire for the job?" Speaking in a way that sounds like work if anyone happens to overhear.

Zarrin spoke without hesitation, "Parvin will help you."

Tomas looked over at the woman at the table and knew not to say anything, but it showed in his face.

Zarrin saw it too and said, "She is as good as anyone at this table."

Being the good soldier Tomas said, "Very well."

"In fact," Zarrin said, "I have looked into the blueprint and I want to share some fascinating information. Each morning people meet in a parking lot near here to catch a bus that makes no other stops until they are on the site. Most are members of the organization while others are civilian contractors. It would be an easy distraction. Do you have other plans ready?"

"Jose and Pedro are out working on them."

"Good, then all is settled." She said as a statement, not a question. "When I see the needs, I will help further to fill in the positions."

She had told the order despite what Tomas may have wanted to say to prove her authority; something she has done several times which had not gone unnoticed. The distraction operation was hers and the way she explained it, was told not for debate. Tomas will make it fit.

"Parvin, take your car and confirm the daily routes of the bus for me. Report your information to Tomas."

"Tomas, my friend. Clear all of Parvin's plans through me. She is valuable and someone I am not yet ready to sacrifice."

Tomas nodded his understanding and left.

Peter, Sarah, and Rafael had stayed up most of the night despite the request for sleep that was not easy under the circumstances. They compiled a list of targets to explore the options. They decided if this were a standard terrorist attack, it would have already happened. They would have used a poor idealistic person from any country and offered compensations to their surviving family. Some are the martyrs we imagine as hard-liner Islamic believers. The truth is most terrorists are recruited from extreme and impoverished areas with a promise of support for the families. They have no education or future of support. It is like the "thug life" in America's projects. Children are raised by single mothers who themselves have no education. They are taught that the government is to blame for all their problems. Yet, they become dependent on the entitlement programs provided from the same government and see no sense in seeking the American dream. They blame those who seek our capitalistic economy with success. They gravitate to anything or any group appearing on their radar that provides them with a feeling of family, security, support, and power.

For a dirt farmer in any third world country who has any semblance of a family to help, to become a homicide bomber for their prospects is hard to refuse. Regardless if you think you are going to have 72 virgins and hang out with Allah, they are still placed under heavy sedation to help them in their journey. Israel is under constant threats of terrorist attacks. They teach their population to watch for the person who does not fit the environment. They will be sweating and appear focused. They will not respond to commands due to audio occlusion. They know that the best option for dealing with this person is a shot that severs the central nervous system. Turn the brain off to prevent the finger pressing the detonator. Therefore, a separate handler equipped with a secondary bomb trigger controls many terrorists in case the "martyr" has second ideas or is stopped. They can detonate the explosives by remote.

Peter and the team have decided that this group are on a specific mission. It is not for intelligence-gathering but one of importance. Otherwise, there would be no need for the dramatics on the border nor to have Humberto killed. They could have been arrested and deported and try again. No, it was not the standard issues; it is something greater. There are no planned trips to the area by the President or other cabinet officials. There are no planned international sporting events. There can only be one target, MacDill Air Force Base, the home of Central and Special Operations Commands.

Peter has always believed that they are Iranian trained based upon their tactics and weapons of choice. Security on base is tight since 9/11. The air and water space are restricted and crash walls installed at the gates. These require all vehicle traffic to negotiate a series of S-curves around the barriers before the gates. It prevents anyone from driving at high speeds through the gates before the security forces can act.

He placed a call. "Hey John, it's Peter."

"What have you got."

"We have been looking at the options and examining the possible targets in the area and we can come up with one hard and numerous soft targets."

"Ok, let's have what is thought so far."

"There are many soft targets like malls and theaters in Tampa. Any one of these would be easy to attack. Then there are all the sports arenas that have some security. There is one hardened target and that is MacDill Air Force Base. It is the home of Central Command for our forces in the Middle East and elsewhere."

"Makes sense, but like you said it is a hardened target. Wouldn't one of the other targets be a better choice for anyone trying to do something?"

"Maybe, but why Tampa? If you were going to hit a soft target like a mall, why not the Mall of the Americas in Minneapolis or The Woodfield Mall in Chicago? You would want somewhere with impact and high damage probabilities. Besides, sending someone into a mall with explosives doesn't require any training or preparations. It has to be MacDill; I just do not know how yet."

"Ok Peter. How do the others feel about this opinion?"

"The same."

"Including Sally?"

"Yes."

"Ok. I will make the calls and get back to you."

He hung up and Peter turned and said to the others, "John is going to make the calls, I guess up the chain."

"We don't have a chain, Peter." Sally replied. "Trust is placed in all of us. Have you not noticed how no one is interfering with your decisions?"

"Yeah, I have. I was wondering how long it was going to take before someone did."

"Well, no one will unless there is a disagreement." She replied.

Peter said, "I have never worked like this before, but I sure do like it. Who will he call?"

"Someone with a direct line to the top. The very top." Rafael said.

Peter's phone rang again, and he answered, listened and closed with, "Roger that."

"Ok then." Peter said. "Let's pack up."

"Where are we going?" asked Rafael.

"We're going to the base."

"You mean near the base, right?" Sarah asked.

"Nope, John has called, and they are expecting us on the base. We will be staying in the visiting officers' quarters, which are assigned to visiting dignitaries or generals. It is a short distance from the home of General Burns, the head of Central Command."

# 33

Jose stopped at several locations around Dale Mabry Highway near the entrance of the main gate to MacDill AFB. He will change locations if he thinks he is standing out. He parks at a McDonald's restaurant watching the activity at the gate. Traffic enters the S-curves and slows down for the armed security police. There are four officers at the gate and two others in a truck off to the side. He noticed there were regular roving patrols around the gate and some walking the perimeter while others were on all-terrain vehicles. He thought the security for the base was tight, but it had to be this way because of the importance of the location. There is another base gate on Bayshore Drive, but it was closed with four security police officers. They too were supplemented with the roving patrols. Jose watched someone park off to the side and walk into the gate security building. They later exited and drove into the base with papers in hand.

It is eleven in the morning and Jose watches as a silver car is directed to the side and parks. Two men and a woman exit and walk inside. Jose moves to his van, grabs a pair of binoculars, and sat in the back where he cannot be seen from the outside. He watches as the three come out and return. The car, white male and female look like the people from yesterday that chased their van. The third person is a Hispanic male. He calls Tomas.

"Tomas, I believe I ran into the man and woman we saw yesterday that drove past the apartments." He is keeping the conversation generic.

"Really." Tomas said. "Did you get a chance to say hello?"

"No, they had driven off before I had a chance to see them and they never saw me. They drove into the gated community where I was having lunch."

"They must have a key to the gate."

"They had to go inside the office first." Jose replied.

"Are you sure it's the same couple?"

"Not sure but they and their car match. There is another guy with them but he is Hispanic."

"Interesting. Why don't you hang around and see if you can catch them when they leave?"

They both hung up. Tomas doesn't like it as he is not a believer in coincidence.

"Why are the same people who chased us yesterday arriving at our target?" He thought to himself. "Is it possible that Humberto had been briefed by someone before he left?"

But he knew Humberto had the least information of them all and he let the thought pass. Speaking to himself, "I still do not like it and I will not tell any of this to Zarrin. I do not want her to panic and call this operation off."

He saw her with his Latin male superiority even though he knew he would never tell her such words himself, for now. He was waiting to hear from Parvin and Pedro. He knew Pedro would be the longest considering the time on water.

Later, Parvin called Tomas and asked if he would like coffee.

"Sure," he said, "where?"

"In the lobby, I am waiting."

They met and sat in the plush chairs off the "continental breakfast area" of the room. Parvin explained how every morning at 6:30 AM; the Defense personnel gathers and waits for the bus to go to the base.

"I have already discussed this with her." He knew she meant Zarrin. "I was told to let you know that it is an excellent choice for a surprise. We will keep providing you with what you will need to complete it."

Tomas knew she meant a detonator for the C4. He was more convinced than ever that he had made the correct assumption not to anger Zarrin. She is well placed.

"We will be providing you with additional information soon about the schedule of our guest of honor." She is referring to the commander of the base. His information is provided to allow Tomas to make his final plans since it is still unknown how or what to attack.

"All such people keep a rigorous schedule and hold tight to the times. His house is along the water, facing Tampa Bay. He is home by 7:00 PM and out by 8:00 AM. There are staff members who will sometimes pick him up and drop him off. Within the last day or so, there has been a security car parked a block away. There are police on boats, both military and local enforcing the no entry zone. Two more boats have appeared. This should work in our favor. Also, when the time comes, do not let anyone stand in our way."

Tomas noticed her use of, "our way."

"From what you have said, it sounds like you all have been observing the area a while and may join us for the surprise."

"You will be told when all is decided."

"I thought I was doing the deciding, but it sounds as though there are others inside."

"Why yes, yes you are Tomas. I will be in touch."

"Wait." Tomas said, thinking now is not the time to delay the knowledge he has and to spread his wings a little.

"The people who chased us after Humberto left, they were seen entering the base a few hours ago. My source has not let me know that they have left."

She thought a moment and walked out of the hotel.

# 34

The team was escorted to their new housing in the Visiting Officers Quarters or VOQ. The VOQ's are divided like hotels by expense, which equates to rank. The standard rooms are for enlisted personnel up to the suites used by visiting generals. The team had a suite so they could remain together. They can see General Burns home from the room. There is a knock at the door as they settled in and separated into different rooms to work. Peter answered and met with a young Air Force Captain, William Sears with the Office of Special Investigations or OSI. The OSI is a federal law enforcement agency that reports to the Secretary of the Air Force. They conduct criminal investigations, counterespionage, and protective services worldwide.

After a brief introduction, Captain Sears entered and sat in the living room.

"I am sorry for the interruption sir, but I was briefed that we should make your stay here comfortable. I do not know why you are here or who you are, work for, or anything else."

Smiling as a former military man himself, Peter can only imagine what the young Captain is thinking.

"Captain Sears, I can only tell you that we are not with the military."

He had suspected it and was sure that they are an OGA, or Other Government Agency. This means the CIA.

Peter continued, "We have credible evidence of suspected activity that could be directed to the base."

"That explains the reason for the heightened security alerts. They told us to watch for any unusual activities, but we don't know of anything specific. Is there any other information you can share with me?"

"Nothing right now, if I can get a phone number where I can reach you it would be helpful."

The Captain got up to leave writing his number down. He had learned nothing, but at least they each had a contact on base.

"Mr. Berk. I've worked with spooks," the slang name given to CIA operatives, "and there is a tendency to keep info in tight."

"Captain. I know where you're going. When I know something, you'll know. This is a defensive operation for now while we gather information. It may not even happen. But I assure you I will contact you when I know anything specific."

"Thank you, sir." Captain Sears said as he left the room.

"Alright everybody." Peter said. "What do we have? Has anybody been able to reach out and discover any other information?"

Sarah was on the phone as she came out of her room. "Thanks, and let me know if anything is found."

"Hey guys." She said. "That was our analyst in Miami. The Florida Highway Patrol worked an abandoned vehicle fire the other night on the entrance ramp from Highway 60 in Brandon to southbound I-75. There are no witnesses how the van got there or where the driver left the area. It was a minivan with no plates. It was arson because of the speed and intensity of the burn. No information was found inside. We have requested and they are assigning someone to examine the van further for a confidential VIN number."

Peter sat there for a moment. "In Brandon going southbound. Has there been any other activity involving a similar van anywhere in the area?"

"None reported by any agency." She answered.

Peter thinking a loud said, "What is around there? How could the vehicle occupants be picked up? What about hotels in the vicinity? If they walked away, what businesses are nearby? Check for any stolen vehicle reports from that night to noon the next day close enough for someone to walk."

Rafael said, "I'll go over to the area tomorrow and check it out with the authorities."

The next day, Rafael drove to the scene of the fire. The location is obvious because of the large burn mark in the asphalt. The van burnt down fast. Taught to always place himself in the shoes of the opponent, the first option is to have someone standing by to drive you out of the area. Without a witness and the report said there were none, there is no way to clear that choice. The second is to walk out of the area. If this was deliberate, the location was well chosen. No one can see what is happening without driving past. To the south was an overpass. Looking at a map he sees it is Lumsden Road. The person could walk through the brush and walk away from the scene. Rafael walked to the south along the shoulder to the edge of the overpass and turns west. He walks a straight line that will cross the path of anyone walking to the crossroad from the scene. About 100 feet in he sees what he was looking for, footprints and bent weeds. He measures the prints and looks back to where they had come; from the rear of the burn location. He follows them to the road and steps onto the shoulder of Lumsden Road. He looks both east and west. The only direction that had growth was east. He returns to his car and checks his GPS. Driving south and exiting to north Highway 301, it intersected with Causeway Boulevard. His GPS told him to turn right and the road changes names to Lumsden Road. He continues east and travels over the overpass of the interstate where the van had burnt. He sees a Costco to the right and a Walmart to the left and the Brandon Mall behind Walmart. He calls their analyst and asked for information of stolen cars and hotels in the vicinity that included the Brandon mall.

The analyst called him back and said that night there were four cars and one van stolen from that area. Malls and shopping strip centers are always targets for thieves.

"A van? Give me the information."

He was told of a white van stolen from the Walmart parking lot within walking distance of the fire.

Rafael called Peter and filled him in. "I like the van description."

"So do I. They always like to stick with something familiar. Let's put that information out and see what we come up with. I'll have Sarah switch gears to the hotels in the area."

"Roger that."

# 35

Peter received an email from John that said a statewide BOLO or Be On The Look Out, was placed on the van with a special notice to "approach with caution, occupants possibly armed and dangerous." Peter shows it to Sarah as they walked into the Command Operations building to meet with General Burns.

"You can have a seat over there." Sgt. Wright directed them. "The General said he will meet with you in a moment."

Peter looked at Sarah as they entered the waiting room. "I knew this was how it was going to be."

Sarah smiles and asked, "What are you talking about? We just got here?"

"You'll see. It has and I guess will always be the same. If we had not flanked his position, he would have been waiting for us.

"What do you mean?"

"He was contacted by someone higher and told instead of going straight to him. This is his base and we are not military brass. We are OGA's to him, no one important. There is always this power and ego game that gets people hurt through either a lack of or refusal to act."

"Come on Peter, relax. It's no big deal. He is a busy man."

"Ok, we'll see."

Thirty minutes later, Peter looked at her and smiled. Sarah said nothing but was starting to think he could be right.

Parvin arrived in the parking lot of Home Depot, dressed in a gym outfit. Tomas is there waiting with Jose after receiving a call to meet her for lunch. Jose had returned not to draw attention by staying too long near the gate. He picked up Tomas and drove him down the street for the meeting. She sprang from her white Suburban, smiled, and waved as she trotted over to the van wearing a backpack. Tomas knew she was playing a game of recognition in case anyone was watching it would not appear odd.

She enters the van, gave him the backpack and said, "Your other tools are in a suitcase in the back of my car. I was told to tell you to speed up the plan and check out of the hotel. You can take my car, here are the keys."

"Where will you return the van?" Tomas asked.

"I will not. Our sources say they are already looking for it. My car is clean and has more than enough room inside."

Tomas sat in silence for a moment thinking. He hates when plans involving him are made without his knowing.

"She also said," indicating the higher authority of Zarrin, "To tell you it is time to move underground. There appears to be additional activities taking place. No more problems. You know how to contact us when finished. Let's go."

Tomas and Jose exited the van. Jose is watching Tomas who is ready to explode.

"Let's go Tomas. Do not worry about it." He stopped as Tomas stared at him. His eyes searing through his own.

"Do not say another word!" as he walked to the Chevrolet and got inside. He handed Jose the keys.

"Drive to the hotel. We will pack up and move onto the boat with Pedro."

Tomas opens the backpack and sees it is filled with cash. He knows the detonators for the explosives and weapons are in the trunk.

Parvin drives from the restaurant smiling with the thought of again talking down to a man. Especially one who thinks so high of himself. Parvin enjoys this bit of independence of having the strict walls of Islam brought down and allowing her freedoms she has never known. She could get used to life here. She has long heard stories of others who came to America with ideas of destruction and becoming swayed to the side of freedom. Then she thought back to her training that was designed to prevent such thoughts.

"Freedom is in the mind of the individual. The mind of the individual is inside the cause. The cause is built with the minds of all who believe, which together has created our opportunity for a jihad against the infidels."

She is driving to a nearby apartment complex. It is a gated community where she had noticed the gates left open during the busy times of the day. Many gated communities keep their gates open during peak hours, so the residents can come and go. It is an ideal place to leave the van and she can Uber back to their hotel. The phone rang and it startled her. She swerves and realizes that she is speeding. She cursed aloud realizing her mistake. She looks behind her as the traffic stopped ahead. Turning back around she sees the traffic and slams on the brakes. Her phone slides into the floorboard as the van comes to a stop. Beside her to the right is a Hillsborough County Sheriff's Office patrol car. Her behavior goes into training mode as she tries to hide her nerves, smiles and shrugs her shoulders as if to say, "I'm sorry."

The deputy smiles back and waits for her to continue. He runs the tag and sees that it appears correct but registered to an older couple from the other coast near Daytona. The woman looks foreign and dressed in clothes for the gym. Her appearance says luxury, not driving this van. He decides to stop her and check on the vehicle. Besides, there was a BOLO for a white van.

He pulls in behind her and activates his emergency equipment. Parvin sees the lights and contemplates running for a second before pulling to the side and stopping. Again, she goes into training mode as she unzips her top a little further to expose more of her breast. She sees her phone on the floorboard and cannot reach it without getting out of her seat and climbing to the other side. This action could be perceived as suspicious and lead to a search. She sits and waits. She hears the car door of the officer slam and she watches through her side view mirror as he approaches the driver's window. A tactical mistake she thinks to herself knowing that the passenger's side offers greater protections.

"Good afternoon, ma'am. I am Deputy Wilson of the Hillsborough County Sheriff's Office. I need to see your driver's license, registration, and insurance for the vehicle please."

"What did I do wrong officer? I do not understand good English." she replies smiling.

"You almost had an accident back there and I want to make sure you are alright. License and registration please."

She hands him a business card from Denny's restaurant and said, "My phone fall on floor. I am sorry, I was trying to get to my phone."

"I understand ma'am, can I see your driver's license?" As he said this, he pulls out a notepad and begins writing down the VIN number to the van.

Parvin knows she could be in trouble if he runs that number and she points to her phone and said, "Please officer, you get for me? My papers in there I think." Pointing now at the glove box.

"Sure, one moment."

He was smiling for several reasons but none more than the sight of her olive-skinned breast. He cannot take his eyes from her cleavage. He walks around the front of the van. Parvin is smiling and acting coy. It is a teasing game that both men and women find irresistible. He reaches the other side and opens the door. She is leaning toward him smiling flirtatiously. The actions have removed all his tactical senses and turned him into a puppet. That could change in an instant and she knows it. She has to act before this goes any further. She glances around and brought her right hand up from between the seats. It appears she is using the arm for support but is holding a Glock model 27 compact .40 caliber handgun. The deputy himself determines the next action. He glances over and sees the gun as she raises it towards him. He responds as anyone does in that instant of realized fear. He brings his arms up as if trying to direct her actions to stop. He takes one-step back as she yells, "Stop and you will not be hurt!"

He is still bending over and starts to pull away while drawing his own weapon as she fires three fast rounds. The first-round travels over and behind his bullet resistant vest and enters his upper chest with no exit. The second-round hits him in the left cheek and exits the back of his head. The third round is a miss caused by the impacts of the first two rounds on his body. Deputy Wilson dies within moments.

# 36

General Burns is the four-star in charge of Central Command and he came out of a side room and approached Peter and Sarah.

"I do not have a lot of time so let's get to the point." He exclaimed.

"General, would this be better elsewhere maybe?" Sarah asked.

"This is good. You can fill me in on specifics and give details to Colonel Franken. He's my chief of staff."

Peter said, "Sir I don't think you understand the seriousness of the information we have for you, could we please…"

The general cut him off and Peter knew those stars were going to have to display who was in charge.

"Mark, let me explain…"

"It's Peter, General, Peter Berk, not Mark."

"Ok Peter Berk, the issue here is you do not understand that I am a busy man in charge of this entire base and overseas operations in the Middle East."

"Oh, I understand alright General."

"No, I don't think you do. Get to the information you have now or let Colonel Franken know later."

Sarah knew it was time for her to become involved. This was looking like a couple of bulls pushing and puffing against each other.

"General, we have reasons to believe that the base is being targeted for some type of action."

"This is Central Command; we are always targeted from some radical somewhere. We have all the personnel and measures in place. I received a call from the Defense Secretary's office and told to accommodate you and that is what I am doing. Should you have any other issues, take them up with Colonel Franken. If you will excuse me."

General Burns turned to walk away. "General." Sarah said as Peter grabbed her arm. He never slowed or showed any sign of hearing or caring what she had to say.

"It is as I said." Peter said. "We are on our own unless we can convince Colonel Franken of a few issues. I am sure the General has informed him to short leash us."

Sarah stood for a moment and looked at Peter who was also starting to walk out in the opposite direction. "Hey! What's next?"

"Back to the VOQ and call Captain Sears."

"I thought Burns said to check with Colonel Franken for everything."

"He did. which is why we are not going through him. Remember, he is his Chief of Staff and must be a confidant. Anything we say to him he will clear through Burns."

Captain Sears answered on the second ring.

"Hey Captain, Peter Berk."

"Hello Mr. Berk, how can I help you?"

"Listen, we just left General Burns and I understand that there may be a home vacated near his residence."

Sarah is staring at him but not saying a word to see where this is going.

After a brief hesitation, Sears said, "Well, yes. There is ah, the Weller home that is General Weller's home. It is next door, ah, did General Burns say something about…"

Peter cut him off, "Yes he did, and the sooner we can get out of the VOQ and into the Weller home the better."

"Did the General authorize this Mr. Berk?"

"Listen Captain. I understand as a former military officer myself that the rank of Captain can be precarious, but if I have to call back and forth between Colonel Franken so he can interrupt the General who is busy running a war because Captain Sears wants to double check every damn command, we are not going to get anywhere."

"Yes Sir, Mr. Berk. I do understand and I was told to give you any help you asked for." The last part said as if he was starting to talk to himself in a lower voice.

"Great Captain, can we get picked up in about an hour for the transfer?"

"Yes sir. I will be there."

"Good. I also want to discuss some issues that may be occurring."

He hung up and looked at Sarah who was still staring at him as she smiled and said, "When did Burns tell us we can move?"

"He didn't, but he never told us we couldn't. I did not lie to Sears."

"Yes, you did. Not telling the truth or leaving out the truth is the same thing, but I like it. Why do you want to move there anyway?"

"It's a hunch. What else could be the target here? The base is enormous and well protected. When we think about targets, will they be hard or soft?"

"Softer the better as long as they are valuable." She replied.

"What is softer out here, the buildings, or the leaders in charge?"

Sarah did not respond but it was obvious she was thinking.

# 37

Parvin accelerates into traffic. She sees other drivers stop and run to help the downed officer. This causes a traffic jam as she pulls away from the scene.

"Slow down!" she says to herself repeating training commands for this type of scenario. "Do not attract attention to yourself. Watch traffic behind you and try to recognize any vehicles for tails. Time to get rid of the van. Stop somewhere. Wipe it all down. Pull the plate if you have time."

"Get off the main road!" She yells as she turned right onto the next road that was four lanes. She drives up to the next light and sees traffic waiting on the signal to change. She looks in the mirror at the drivers in cars behind her for unusual behaviors. She sees several women in one talking and laughing. A man in another looking at his phone and reading text. A work truck with the right front passenger sleeping. Three cars back in her lane is a silver Ford. The man is talking on the phone, but his behaviors are different. He looks serious and concerned, not smiling and looking around as if trying to find street names or landmarks.

Parvin looks ahead and decides to make another turn to see if the car is following her. In a usual situation, she would change lanes and turn left or make a U-turn to see if anyone followed. This situation is different. She cannot afford to draw more attention in case he was not following her.

The light changed and she made it to the intersection. She did not use her blinker and turned right. She watches as the Ford turns with her. Hearing the sirens of emergency vehicles speeding to the scene; to her or both, Parvin cannot wait any longer. She has to do something and thinks of turning into a driveway, but he could drive past without stopping and describe her location or block her in. She made a left turn onto the next road and slowed. If he follows her, this will place his driver's window at an angle to her side of the van. He did follow. She hit the brakes, threw the van into reverse, and accelerates. As the other driver is coming out of the turn, he sees the van and stops. There is nowhere for him to go. The van collides hard with his car and activates his air bags. Stunned by the impacts, he has a momentary streak of pain on the left side of his head and then nothing.

Parvin is standing next to the driver's window. The shot struck the man in the left temple. There is no doubt he is dead. Now is the time to leave the van and flee on foot before more people show up. She turns and sees the officers. During the intensity of the encounter two sheriffs' car and a State Trooper arrived at the scene blocking two of her directions. She tries to run as the gunfire breaks out. The officers, having seen her execute the man did not need any reasons not to prevent her escape.

Armed with AR15's and shotguns, the officers have her covered. She has nowhere to run except to use the van as protection. The range of the shotgun and the rifles have her defeated. She hears more sirens as more police from various agencies are responding. It is one thing to kill, but to kill a police officer brings everyone with a badge regardless of the agency. Parvin looks around to decide whether to fight or surrender. Surrender is not part of her training, but neither is a senseless fight. She understands the damages she can inflict upon the enemy. She pulls out her shirt to show she is unarmed, her breast still partially exposed from the flirtation with the deputy. She lays down her gun and raises her arms.

More units arrive and they approach her at gunpoint.

"Watch your crossfire." the Trooper called out to the others as they approach in a circular fashion.

As the officers get close, one of them grabs her arms. She starts a gag reflex and tries to throw up causing the others to pause. This gives Parvin the instant needed as she turns and lunges on the officer driving her thumb into his left eye. He screams and falls backwards, dropping his weapon. She follows him screaming, "Allah Akbar!" She grabs the weapon and one of the officers fires a shot that created a multitude of shots as she tries to fire back. One of the rounds strike the officer who is on the ground, yet most hit her. She lays and smiles to the sky and dies.

# 38

Peter and Sarah meet with Captain Sears at the waterfront house that faces east and is west of the main perimeter road; Bayshore Blvd. MacDill Air Force base is on the end of a peninsula with most of the base bordered by water. General Burns' home faces Tampa Bay off the Boulevard that runs along the entire east coastline. A small wall separates the residence from the traffic of the boulevard and blocks some of the winds that comes across in the winter from the north and east. Peter and Sarah settle into the Weller home that is a few hundred feet north of an even larger home and also faces the bay.

"Thanks Captain, this will do fine. Is that the Burns' residence?" Peter said pointing to the large house to the south.

"Yes sir, it is. Let me know if there is anything I can do for you. Now about the information you mentioned."

Peter's phone went off. He looks at the screen and sees it is Rafael and tells everyone, "Give me a moment."

He answered the phone and walks into the kitchen, "Rafi, what's up."

"You guys see what's happening in Brandon right now?"

"No. We've been busy, what's going on?"

At the same time, he leans back out and tells the others to turn on the television, local news.

Rafael explained how he was following up on the stolen van from the mall and the hotels in the area and how a deputy stopped a van with a female driver who shot and killed him. She fled the scene but was followed by a witness to an area a mile away and she ambushed him before captured by police.

"Ambushed who?" Peter said as he interrupts to try to keep the facts straight.

Rafael paused a moment and said, "The witness. She killed the witness who was following her."

"Did they catch her?"

"Yes and no." Rafael replied and went on to explain how she attacked one of the deputies before she was shot and killed from the other officers who also shot an injured officer in the confusion. "He is in serious condition at Tampa General Hospital."

He hesitated to let Peter soak in the information and then said, "Guess what she yelled out at the height of the encounter?"

"What?"

"Allahu Akbar. Oh, and one other thing. The van she was driving is the one stolen from the Brandon Walmart."

"You're sure it is the van stolen the same night the other van was destroyed?"

"Positive and more."

"What?"

"Got a call a little while ago from a Tampa Trooper from their Bureau of Criminal Investigations and Intelligence who specializes in vehicle identifications. He told me that the burnt van was bought near Las Cruces, New Mexico by one Javier Sanchez."

"Have someone go there and follow up on the purchase." Peter said.

"Already on it. I called and an officer is going there to pull the papers, addresses, identifications, etc. Should have a copy of his driver's license soon from the New Mexico State Police. I'm sure it will all be fake."

"Great. Let me know what you get back. Tell me more on this dead girl from the shootout."

"No ID on her and we are checking the van for clues. County crime technicians will process the scene and the Florida Department of Law Enforcement or FDLE will take lead on the shooting and assisted by the sheriff's office."

"Thanks Rafi, stay on it and keep me filled in. We have a home to move into out here, so call on your way and I'll give you instructions from our end."

Peter filled Sarah and Captain Sears on the events with the van and the info in New Mexico. Later that day they received the information they had been waiting on. The car lot did not have exterior cameras. A copy of a driver's license issued to Javier Sanchez arrived, but it was not going to help. New Mexico State Troopers went by the listed address and found it to be an empty lot. They then went to the address listed for the real Javier Sanchez based on his driver's license number and found him to be unrelated and his whereabouts at the time verified through his employer.

Peter called John Hatfield in Miami and filled him in on the changing events.

"So, what do you think? What's your gut feeling on things Peter?"

"I believe that whatever is going to happen will be here at MacDill AFB. We have the Iranians training in Venezuela, Tomas or Fauzi Guerra, a confirmed terrorist from the CIA, our only informant with information murdered going to meet Fauzi, and now some deranged female terrorist killing herself to avoid arrest after killing a deputy and witness and nearly killing another officer. They have been here a while and could have done anything already but haven't. They're going after MacDill."

"Tough target but I can see the psychological advantages it would have. I'll start moving some assets to your area for a QRF if needed." John responded.

A Quick Reaction Force or a QRF, is a specially trained team chosen for their skill sets from the military. Many of them are former SEAL and DELTA operators.

They can be activated and airborne within 20 minutes to assault a target. Since Peter was certain the target was MacDill, having them ready in the area would save the hour flight out of Miami.

"Sounds good to me." Peter said.

"Keep me informed. Oh yeah, I forgot to ask. How's your communications with General Burns going?"

"How do you think?"

"I can make another call."

"No, not yet. Push too hard and he may really dig his heels in. You know how they are. They all get this God complex whenever they take over a command."

"Alright, but you know it only takes a call."

"We'll be alright for now. I'll let you know if I need an extra push."

They hung up. Peter looks over at Sarah who was surveying the new residence.

"Give me a full layout of MacDill showing areas of weakness and vulnerabilities. Look over the base as if it was you considering the attack. We need to see how we would do this and maybe that will give us the clues needed to see how they will."

"Is there anything specific you want me to focus on?" Sarah asked.

"Everything. Look at everything as a target and prioritize from there."

# 39

Tomas and Jose packed up and spent time cleaning any hint of themselves from the room. They did not think anyone would trace them back to the location, but never take any chances. If you have the time, prepare; something they were taught. They walk to the parking lot and Jose drove the Chevrolet Suburban left by Parvin. Tomas receives a text message from Zarrin as they drive onto the highway.

The text read, "Just leaving work for a late lunch with that red-hot girl from accounting. Why do you meet us at the Sheraton Sabal Park?" The words were not perfect as the first language of any writer or speaker overrides the second. But since it is in a text message, it would never draw attention. Texting has its own set of words and unique phrases like shorthand.

"Pull over in the next parking lot and get directions to a Sheraton hotel in Sabal Park." Tomas said to Jose. "When you get the directions start driving there. Our friends have a problem. They want to meet."

Stopping, Jose is looking at Google Maps on his phone said, "Got it, we will be there in about 10 minutes."

"Don't rush. I want to look over the area."

Zarrin had sent Tomas a code for trouble by including the phrase "red-hot girl" in the message. He looked up the Google satellite images for the location and began to take in the surrounding area, entrances and exits, side roads, wooded lots, and directions. These are all precautions he has to take in this business. He always checks the area even when meeting his "own" people. There are no friends amongst thieves and killers, regardless of the cause.

They arrive in the parking lot of the Sheraton and drive slowly while scanning the area. They park in the back after driving through the lot, got out and walk towards the building. They both notice a man step from the front of the hotel and walk towards them. Tension grew within Tomas.

Looking over to Jose he says, "Don't question me why, say 'Ok I will meet you inside' when I stop. Laugh a little if you understand."

Jose chuckled showing understanding but was increasing his awareness knowing things are done for a reason.

Tomas stops and Jose stopped a step ahead as Tomas said, "I left something in the car."

"Ok. I'll meet you inside." Jose responded on cue and turned to continue walking.

Tomas walks towards the car looking back when he thought Jose would pass the other guy walking towards them. If something was wrong, Jose will be on the receiving end thus allowing him to escape.

They walk past each other and make eye contact, but nothing happened. Jose slowed and looked back at Tomas who waved him to the car. The other man got on the phone and a moment later, a BMW pull up to Tomas. Tense and prepared to grab a gun he watches as the right rear window with dark tint came down and he saw Zarrin sitting in the back seat. She looked out and said, "Get in front."

Tomas followed the instructions as Jose watched them drive out of the lot. He returned to the Suburban and saw the other man walk to the back edge of the parking lot and enter the passenger's side of a car.

Tomas glances around the car as he got in and noticed the driver and another male in the rear seat with Zarrin.

"What is going on that we have to meet like this, again?" He said to show a little disgust with her. "I thought you wanted to advance the operation."

"Shut up and fucking listen to me!" Zarrin screamed out. "I should kill you here and now!"

Tomas, not used to being talked to like this from men, much less a woman starts to turn red with anger but knew he was unable to say anything right now. He was at a distinct disadvantage.

After a second, he said, "What is wrong Zarrin, I do not understand your anger. You sent me the trouble code and now I am here. You talk to me this way and it is you that is angry?"

Ignoring him Zarrin says, "What happened at the vehicle exchange with Parvin?"

"Nothing. Did she say that something went wrong?"

She responds with a low deep growl of a voice as she tries to control her temper, "No she cannot say anything because she is dead!"

"What?" Tomas said shocked. "What happened? We exchanged vehicles and we each left the parking lot."

"She was stopped after leaving and was murdered by the police! Did you see anything or anyone following you?"

"No, no one. We were not followed." He said with confidence before almost saying the wrong thing. "If anyone was followed..."

He stopped short of saying it as Zarrin told the driver, "Turn here."

They turn right into an industrial center, pull into a parking spot at an abandoned building and Zarrin leans forward and said to Tomas. "Go ahead you fool, say it. Blame another who I trust with my life that is dead and I will crush you right here and feed you to the alligators."

Tomas knew his place but also knew this woman was dead the first chance he got when this operation was over. He said nothing. Looking out the window he sees a pond behind several empty buildings; a product of the failed economy and housing markets suffered a few years earlier as he gathers his thoughts. There are signs around the edge of the pond. One read "No fishing, wading, or swimming." The other explained the first, "Do not feed or molest the alligators."

With careful words he said, "I was not aware Parvin had run into this problem. I am sorry for her loss and will say a prayer to Allah for a safe journey for her soul."

He hesitates a moment and then said, "I can assure you that neither she nor us were followed. We are all too good and too well trained to not see that. I know she was a great soldier for the cause as well, for she would not be assigned to you. Someone of foremost importance."

Tomas was speaking with caution yet seething with anger from inside. He continues as his words were calming her.

"Sometimes things happen that is out of our control. Humberto could no longer be trusted, and we had to get rid of our transportation that night. You are the one who helped us, and I say watch their news. American reporters like to tell the story for their own self-interest instead of reporting the facts. They do not care who is hurt if they get credit for breaking a news story. Soon we will know the truth because they will tell us."

Zarrin sat silent. She was watching his reactions to the information. He did appear surprised; even though she knew he was a trained professional and may never reveal a true emotion. Zarrin herself was surprised at the level of concern she was feeling. But Parvin was more than an asset to her. She was a dedicated assistant even when they shared the same bed. A relationship known to no one and kept that way. Islam will never accept these acts regardless of her connections. She often wondered about the hypocrisy of the faith that was so strict that it forced its followers to lie about simple issues. In strict Islam, there is no room for moderates.

"We knew from listening to their police networks that they were looking for the van. This is why I sent Parvin to you, to help further the cause and prevent you from experiencing the same before having the opportunity to complete the mission."

"We are all working toward a great conclusion and I am grateful that you are over watching us." Tomas said.

Zarrin smiled as he twisted the words, common in Spanish when translated to English. She said, "I have been told to send you away for a while."

Tomas starts to object, but she stops him. "This is not up for argument. Things are heated here, and they are going to be on high alert. If we give it some time, they will become sloppy. They are not dedicated as we are. When they have to be alert for too long, they get careless and will back off again. It is then we shall strike when they are tired and have exhausted their resources on futile vigilance. It will not take long. We will wait one week. Can your Captain take care of the boat alone for a while?"

"I will let him know. He is good at what he does." Tomas replied.

"Good. I want you and Jose to travel across the state to keep out of the area in case they know who they are looking for."

"If they knew, would they not put out alerts throughout the country?"

"Yes, but as you say, we will monitor the police radios and news broadcast for any and all reports. We have found that the further from the area, the less they will look for you. Consider the Flagler Beach area north of Daytona and south of St. Augustine. It is several hours away and on the other coast. I have been to this area before. You will be fine there, and I will get in touch with you later. It will not take long before they start getting careless again. Do nothing that will attract any attention. Another mistake and we all will be shamed, and you will pay the price."

Tomas was driven back to the hotel and dropped off. As he walks back to the Suburban, he sees a car in the last row start up and leave with two men inside.

"They are always watching." He thought to himself.

"What happened, what's going on? I think that guy was watching us." Jose tells him as Tomas enters the Suburban.

"Drive up to Interstate 4, we are leaving town for a while. I will explain this later. I need to call Pedro."

"Zarrin called and told the man on the other end, "Watch them and report to me." She hung up the phone not trusting in coincidences.

Tomas calls Pedro and says, "Listen my friend. There is a change in plans. When

the situation gets better, I will get in touch with you. Will you be ok awhile longer?

"Yes. Nothing to worry about here."

"Good. Call if you need anything. I will keep you updated on when we will get back. Keep doing the work you have."

Knowing Tomas was referring to scouting the shorelines and mapping he said, "Ok, I will talk to you soon."

# 40

Peter text Rafael the address of the house and everyone met inside after he arrived. They had already briefed Captain Sears on the murders earlier today involving Parvin, yet they still had not identified her. They were certain she had a connection with an event to take place on the base but did not know what or when that event would be. Captain Sears had increased the security on the base by placing more police personnel at both gates, reduced entrances to the main gate only and requiring verification of all guests for their business purposes and increased the patrol boats that were watching all the sea routes to the base.

"You do know," Captain Sears said. "That until you have something I can take up the chain this will not receive complete backing. There are too many upper brass asses here to listen to hunches which may interrupt their daily events."

That last part had slipped out and Sears starts to apologize when Peter said, "No need to say anything Captain. I can imagine what it must be like stationed where a Colonel is low on the scale of importance. I was army."

"Yeah, it does get a little hairy around here and if you have not noticed, neither Major Simmons nor Colonel Bolton, my commanders on base have been in touch with you. I report to Major Simmons, and he gave me tacit approval to take steps based on the intelligence we receive. So far, we have not done anything considered unusual. I wish we had more marine coverage."

Since 9/11, the waters around MacDill AFB have been restricted to military personnel, an act that frustrated the hundreds of civilian anglers who enjoyed sport fishing around the base. With the help of the Florida State Fish and Wildlife Service, no boat traffic is allowed within this restricted waterway. Several boats are approached each week and notified to leave the area. But with miles of coastline to patrol, the task is difficult with so few assets.

"What do we do now?" Rafael asked.

Peter responded, "It's up to them. There is not much we can do but wait. We don't have much information to work with, so the next move is theirs. We have followed up on each possibility. We can do more if Interpol, NSA, CIA or someone gets proof positive of who this girl was that killed the officer. Till then, wait and retrace our steps to be sure we have not missed something. Sarah what have you got planned already?"

Sarah has been working on her assault plan of the base said, "As I see it, there are only two vehicle and pedestrian gates. They each have concrete pillars laid out in a "S" formation to prevent anyone from rushing the gates. I understand that Captain Sears has doubled the guards at each of these and closed the Bayshore gate, is that right?"

"Yes ma'am, it is." Capt. Sears replied.

"We have this fence along the northern edge of the base," pointing to a map. "Have any of you been to El Paso?" she asked.

They all said "yes" except Captain Sears.

"Ok, in El Paso, the Border Patrol has a system in place called 'Hold the Line'. What they have done is place a border agent every hundred feet or so as a physical and visual deterrence to cross in that area. It has been effective and reduced the illegal crossings from hundreds per night to just a couple. It is much easier to go east or west around El Paso than try there. Do you see where we are going with this?"

"What you're suggesting Miss Jenkins," Captain Sears said. "Is, we place someone every hundred feet?"

"No, you do not have to do that. The difference is in El Paso, there are many sight barriers such as dunes, hills, trees or brush, etc. Here there is nothing. Since this is an air base, as with all airports, the inside perimeter is kept open and cleared. A couple of people can cover a lot of territory. I assume that there are already seismic sensors in the ground on the base side of the barrier fence. Just as on the border, placed so that if someone walks within a certain distance of that sensor it registers the ground movement of the person and signals the activity. But by the time someone sets it off, they have already moved past it and we are left with trying to track the person down."

Captain Sears said nothing, so Sarah interpreted that as meaning "yes" to the sensors.

"What I am saying is that we have a Humvee with two soldiers placed several hundred yards behind the sensor wall and spaced out far enough that they would play a two-part role. One as a visual deterrence and two as a rapid response force to take immediate action until re-enforcements arrive."

"I like it so far." Peter said. "Captain, do you see any areas of improvement or suggestions?"

"No, I do not. With about 10 vehicles, two personnel each, we could effectively cover the entire northern land routes to the base."

"One other thing Captain." Rafael spoke up. "Be sure that each man is briefed on the importance of the job and that they are armed."

"Of course, no problem." Sears answered.

Rafael and the others had been in too many areas of the country during the deployment of National Guard troops and States side bases not to ask this question. To others it sounds redundant. "Really? Arm the troops." But few know that most of the weapons they are carrying during these deployments are empty. Unless they are members of the security police forces, they are often unarmed. We can trust them with many things, but not that!"

"What about anything airborne?" Rafael asked.

"I don't think it is feasible because there are too many airports in the vicinity, too much restricted airspace, and too quick to draw the attention of each of these centers. Besides, to cause any actual harm would have to be something like another 9/11 attack."

"One more thing." Sarah said. "We need to have a QRF ready at a moment's notice. Consider their logistics to be anywhere on base within 15 minutes."

Peter spoke up, "A QRF is enroute already. Be here any hour. I meant to tell you that Captain, but we have been busy. I know General Burns was notified from Washington and I'm surprised I haven't heard from him or his Chief of Staff yet."

"Thanks for telling me now. I will notify Major Simmons to move the information up to confirm. We can place them in a hanger here," pointing at the map, "for rapid movement anywhere on base. I will see to their logistical needs. How many people?" Captain Sears asked.

Peter said, "Know when they get here. It will help if we can get some of your people with tactical training assigned to the QRF. They know the base and the fastest routes to any location. Thanks Captain."

Peter is thinking about Captain Sears and how he has not been included in any of the decisions. Keeping people involved even if it is a sense of involvement is the best way to keep them motivated and on your side.

Peter spoke out. "Intel, anything current from our partners? Have there been increases in intercepted chatter?"

Sarah had been keeping track of the reports presented by the NSA, CIA, FBI and the State Department. "Nothing unusual."

"What about the water routes?" Rafael asked.

Sarah flipped through some pages and brought up an aerial view of the base.

"As you can see, water borders two thirds of the base. A water approach is the best approach. If this were my operation, I would choose a water assault. All the facilities are reachable from any of these shore areas on the east side. Marine assets are limited. The difference is with radar from three boats positioned here, here, and here (Pointing to the west, east and southern tips of the base peninsula.) you can monitor any approaching vessels."

She hesitated a moment and said, "Me. If this were mine. I would place swimmers in the water outside of the restricted zone or I would concentrate an assault here (pointing to the upper east side of the beach close to all the buildings and housing areas). By a concentrated assault, I mean one that utilizes all the resources on a single point of weakest resistance to overwhelm my opponent and cut off command and control with confusion."

"Boyd's theory of Fast Transients." Peter spoke up. "But it requires a two-prong attack. A diversion maybe."

"Exactly." Sarah said. "It is the most effective combat measure and has been proven in the Middle East. For a diversion I would start an assault at the gates. Look at the distance from the gates to the target buildings. It is too far to be effective. The assault will be by water if this was my ops."

"Why not a diversionary water attack here." Rafael said pointing at the base marina. "Instead of at the gates. This will concentrate your forces to one arena instead of dividing them."

Sarah responded, "You can. I am betting that this will not be a large assault group, but pockets of assailants. No way a large group can exist here without someone tipping the authorities. The same reason we send in small tactical groups to foreign locations. If we assault only the marine areas, the base will deploy most of its resources to that area. By attacking the gates first and delaying the secondary assault, assets will be deployed to the gates leaving less assistance for the marine assault."

"Wow." Captain Sears said. "I'm impressed but not shocked. As I said earlier. We need more marine assets. I will start making plans as soon as possible."

"We needed all this up yesterday, Captain." Peter spoke up.

"Roger that." Sears responded as he walked out the door.

"Listen up." Peter said after the captain left. "I'm still waiting on the soft target list. I didn't want to say anything with Sears here but I'm leaning towards an assassination attempt."

"On who?" Rafael said.

"Who else. Burns."

"General Burns? I can see that. Hard to see an assault or attack on the base itself. Only thing possible is a statement attack at the gates etc. No way to breach the command centers. I agree with Sarah. Too much distance."

Sarah said. "You hinted to that before so I've been looking at the marine access and that would make sense because the General's house overlooks the water."

Peter, nodding in agreement says, "I know in my bones it will be here and the extra gate security, perimeter patrols, and a QRF force can overcome anything else. It has to be by water and what a morale boost and recruitment poster for these groups to kill the commander of the forces raging war against their homelands."

"We're not going to get what we need in short order. Because of the budget build up, much is not yet available." Sarah said.

Since the end of the last administration, the military is building again after eight years of stagnation. Unfortunately, because of the great needs across all the services, to rebuild that many years of loss is not easy. The rebuilding is a priority, but it will take years to stop the degradation and more years to build up.

"Yeah. Were lucky this hasn't happened sooner. Let's do what we can to stop it if it is to take place here and be ready to move if we find out otherwise."

# 41

Pedro is on the boat at the shrimp docks where he has befriended some of the workers. He spent the last week scouting the area and was told to mark all the locations on a map such as Coast Guard stations and marine patrol offices. He is also finding the ramps used by officers to launch their boats. Most will have a ramp that is convenient to use based upon their routes to and from home. Unlike other officers, they do not report to an office daily and most take their boats home or have a storage arrangement with a marina. This information shows where an outside approach can be made to intervene in an assault and show areas without coverage for an escape.

He is also gathering information about the water restrictions around MacDill AFB. The restricted zones are marked with a border of signpost in the water showing no access. He stays below at the docks out of sight for long stretches of time not to draw attention to himself for not going out fishing. When he does go topside, he is always sure to have dirty hands and clothes to appear as if he is making repairs. The boating business is like the trucking industry. If they are not moving spending money, they are not making money. If you are not catching shrimp, then you cannot afford the cost of the boat. There are many times though that the boat needs repairs and updating to keep up with the rigors of the job in the saltwater environment.

The fishing industry is a tight knit community. Any time you have a group of people willing to make sacrifices and share hardships together, they become close with one another. They also have many who are fleeing from one thing or another and gravitate to the idea of being away at sea for long stretches at a time. No one ask questions and if there are too many of the wrong questions, it is easy to have an "accident".

Returning from another "engine test", Pedro pulls up to the docks and the others on the pier stop and watch.

"Never seen him before." A worker on another boat said.

"Yeah, I have. He's been around. No crew. Seems to be working on the boat." Another deck hand said.

Pedro moved forward to attach a bow line. Another guy on the dock came over, took the aft line, and tied it off.

"Gracias amigo."

The guy waved his hand.

Pedro went below and continued marking his navigational chart of Tampa Bay with ramp locations and Coast Guard stations. He waited until Saturday, packed a bag and included the chart. He walked up the dock early and called a cab to take him to the nearest rental car center. He thought of calling Tomas but assumed other things had happened since he was not staying with him.

Driving a rental car, he traveled to each boat ramp on the chart. He chose Saturday because that was when the most marine police will be on the water. A look at the ramps shows their trucks, trailers, and general patrol areas. He marked these on his chart and marked circular perimeters. Returning the car and another cab ride back to the docks, it is dark, and the dock lights are on. He walks to his boat and hesitates as he approached. Not having the time for standard security equipment, Pedro sprinkled a mat with talcum powder and placed it at the pass through in the railing. Now standing in the dim lit area, he see's footprints leading to the hatch of the cabin. There are no prints on the dock so whoever stepped onto the boat is still there. He moves quietly past the boat to the end of the dock and sits down behind an equipment box.

"Who is on the boat?" he whispers to himself. "Maybe Tomas or Jose has had a change in plans? May be the police?" He reaches into his bag and removes a fish knife; long narrow and sharp. He waits and watches. He sees the water ripple away from his boat. Whoever it is, they are moving around.

Ten minutes pass and he sees a man look out of the cabin. He glances around and moves toward the dock faster than he had arrived; he surmises. The thin young man steps off the boat and walks down the dock passing beneath the lights.

"He's no police." Pedro says to himself as he watches the guy turn right onto a finger pier and onto another shrimp boat and leaving a powdered trail to follow that fades away. "Fucking thief!"

Waiting a few more moments Pedro steps onto his boat and moves the mat. He goes below and sees most things are in place. The boat has not been ransacked as he expected but looked through. He opened a few drawers and noticed a watch was missing. It belonged to Kurt Johnson, the owner of the boat. The last thing he needed was for it to show up at a pawnshop and have a hit by police. Everything turned into a pawnshop is catalogued, reported to police, and the person pawning the item fingerprinted. Even though a missing boat owner and boat from another state are not going to have their belongings catalogued and entered stolen, it still possesses a risk.

"Maybe it is not a bad thing this guy gets fingerprinted for the dead man's jewelry. But if he gets arrested and points out from where he stole the watch, that is bad. Besides. I don't need the police asking questions of this missing boat from Texas." He thinks to himself.

"That could take a while to happen. Worse is if the nosey bastard looked over any of my maps. Everybody hates thieves, especially me." He says aloud.

# 42

Tomas and Jose drive to the east coast of Florida and north on I-95. They exit at SR100 and drive to the Hampton Inn near the highway. They settle into a room. Little is discussed during the trip. Tomas needs to wrap his head around what has happened to Parvin and the threats given him by Zarrin. Even though he was angry, he knew the death of Parvin was a setback. They will be alert.

"What do we do now and how long will this take? What are the others doing? What about Pedro?" Jose asked.

"I told you we are waiting!" He hates to admit it but waiting is the best thing for

now.

"I told them we have to wait if the Americans are on alert. They will get careless

the longer we wait. I suggested we move out of the area to avoid any more mistakes like Parvin made and strike when they are tired of being nervous." Tomas added decision was his to show he is in charge.

"And Zarrin agreed with you? Good. This is good."

Tomas smiled. "We will wait here a little while and move in a few days. If anyone is looking for anything, we will not appear as long-term visitors. Find us a place to eat."

Jose investigated restaurants and found one straight down the highway near the ocean called the Fish Company. He is tired of eating fast food and wants seafood. They drive to the restaurant and select snapper from the display, and had it grilled with sides. They sat outside to watch the area and ate the fresh fish.

"Do we know how we will approach this yet?" Jose asked.

"No but I am working on it. I will know more when we go back, and I have a chance to talk to Pedro. Pay the bill and I will wait in the car."

Tomas stands and walks to the car as Jose pays their bill in cash. Two days later they check out of their hotel and move to the Fairfield Inn further north closer to St Augustine and all the outlet malls so as not to stay in the same place too long and be remembered. They continue to lay low far enough away from Tampa.

Pedro woke before the sun and watched the dock from inside his boat. About 7:45 AM other crew members were moving about the boats, some going out, others fixing nets and cleaning. From the side pier, he sees the thief. He is the only one who walks to the main pier and looks at the boat.

"There you are. Now I have seen you in the light. You are mine." He said aloud.

He watches to see who is leaving and staying for work. A van shows up to take some crewmembers to local stores for shopping. He did not see the man leave. A few minutes later, he saw him with a wheel barrel full of ice walking back to the boat. He will see where this leads.

Pedro keeps working around his boat for the next few days waiting to hear from Tomas and watching the thief. After dinner, he is having a beer, relaxing and watching the dock activity. It is Tuesday and many of the crews have left for an evening out. After midnight, he sees his chance to get the watch back. He moves over to the boat to the right on the finger pier and looks around. He steps on board, moves to the cabin, and enters. A light is on in a lower deck and he hears someone talking. Another voice answers.

"At least two." He thought to himself. He slips the knife out and moves forward.

"It's bullshit that we aren't getting the same split on the take." One crewmember said to the other.

"I know, but they said this is how it starts. I don't like it either, but we have to start out somewhere."

"But 25 percent less! I could understand 10 percent maybe, but 25 percent!"

From the shadows, Pedro watches as the thief is standing sideways in front of him and talking to another to the right and out of sight. Thinking with the scene in place, if he cuts them, there will be blood splattered everywhere and too much to clean up. This will bring the police. He places the knife in his waistband and pulls a fish bat; a short polymer club that looks like a small baseball bat. On the handle end there is a hook to hang on a railing or ladder. Pedro steps from the shadow and hits the thief hard and solid in the head as he looks to the right at the table. The other man yells, jumps, and flails his arms at the unexpected attack. The thief collapses to the ground. The other man stays against the opposite wall and yells, "Wait! What the fuck man! I got no beef with you. We ain't got no money man. I don't even have a wallet."

"It's ok. I got no beef with you. This piece of shit stole my watch." Pedro bent down and pulled the stolen watch from the thieves left wrist. "Here. Come here. Help me take him topside for some air."

"I don't know man." He said in a high-pitched and scared voice. "I don't want to get involved. I think you may have killed Danny."

"Danny? Is that his name? No, he's not dead. I ain't gonna kill him over a watch. He's gonna have a headache for a while. Help me move him up on the deck and tell your boss I had sea justice on this thief, Danny."

"Alright man. I'm real sorry he did that to you."

"Grab his shoulders." Pedro said to the man as Danny moaned a little. "What's your name?"

"Charles, Chuck."

"Ok Chuck. Thanks for helping me out."

They move him up to the back of the deck. The rear deck is dark colored from the years of nets and bloodied fish.

"That's good right here."

"Here? On the deck hold?"

As they bend forward to lay him down, Pedro pulls the fish bat and slams it down onto the back of Chucks head. He collapses next to Danny. Pedro reaches over, turns on the wash-down hose, and starts pouring it on Danny's face. Danny rocks his head back and forth. Pedro wants him awake. He removes the knife and whispers into his ear, "You are going to die thief." He slowly cuts his throat as Danny's eyes widen in terror. The last thing he will ever see is Pedro's smiling face. He then repeats the move with Chuck except quick and without water. He has done him no wrong, so assures he dies fast. Pedro uses the wash-down to flush the blood over the side that will stop once their hearts stop. He moves them to the edge and slips them into the water. "They will float a while." Thinking to himself. "And come in handy later."

When finished rinsing the deck, Pedro walks back to his boat and climbs into the dinghy. He paddles over, ropes the two bodies together, and floats them to his boat. He looks around and seeing no one, pulls the bodies onto the deck. He drags them to the icebox in the hull used to store shrimp and shovels ice over them. Finished, he takes a shower, changes, and drinks another beer. After a good night's sleep, Pedro wakes early and makes coffee. He walks up on the deck and finds several workers from other boats standing outside.

"Good morning." Pedro said.

"Did you see a couple of guys around here last night?"

"Sure. A bunch coming and going."

"Two guys. The young ones from that boat over there." One of them said pointing at the boat on the other side dock on a finger pier.

"Can't tell you if it was them or not but a couple of guys were walking around last night. I paid them no mind with all the work I was trying to get done. What's up? They steal something?"

"No. Don't think so at least. Hate to try and find more crew now."

One of the others said, "Danny was complaining a lot. Maybe he talked Charlie into leaving. I wonder if them two did steal something."

Mental virus planted; a couple of the guys ran over to their boat.

"Hard to find good crew anymore. Good luck." Pedro said and walks back inside.

As he closes the hatch, he heard one of the guy's yells to the others already on the boat, "Anything missing! If it is, I will find those sons of bitches and string them up. Look it over good. I'm coming to look myself."

120

# 43

Peter came out of the bedroom and poured coffee. The others were working on their computers.

"Anything new?" he asked.

"No nothing." Sarah replied.

Rafael spoke up after closing his laptop, "Nothing. I don't get it. All the activity a week ago and then nothing. You think we made a mistake?"

"Hope not." Peter said.

"I still say no." Sarah responds. "I feel it. We are on track and I think they have gone into hiding. Maybe it's the death of their people or the stepped-up measures on base if they are watching. Maybe it's something else but I know we are not wrong. We just don't know when."

"Think about it." Peter said. "If you were running their ops and you had a setback and saw extra steps taken to fortify, what would you do?"

"Same thing. Wait and let the defenses drop or change targets." Rafael said with Sarah nodding in agreement.

"I don't think you can change targets if all the planning is for the original." Peter said. "The logistics are too much."

"That's true. Sarah responded. "Unless you have secondary targets pre-selected to account for this issue.

Rafi says, "I would agree but I also agree that they are small in numbers and goaled with a major statement. The other targets are softer and don't require much planning. They've been here a little while as Humberto told us. My bet is the base."

"If you're right, then let's have Sears put together a counter-surveillance unit outside the gates. Who knows? We might get lucky and see something. Have we spoken to him since the day before yesterday?" Peter asked.

Sarah said, "He called yesterday afternoon for an ops/intel check and I told him no change. The QRF has been in place. They are split and rotating 12-hour shifts of readiness. They were full ready the first few days and started to fatigue. Split in half for 12 hours, each half is ready in minutes while the other is down resting, chow, etc. I'll contact him and ask about the counter unit."

Peter took a sip of coffee and said, "Fatigued. We are all waiting and getting fatigued."

"Wait and let the defenses drop." Rafael repeated.

"Any information on the extra marine units?" Peter asked.

Rafael said, "None from the military. Local Sheriff's office and city has offered some of their units to supplement. FBI said they could have their black boats with an HRT or Hostage Rescue Team in place in another 24 to 36 hours. Flying them in from Virginia. Temporary trailer housing is being arranged at the marina now, so they are on station and ready."

Peter looks at Sarah as he sits down across from her, "What about it? Still looking at possible targets?"

"Yeah, I have. I keep looking over options. I want to give every one of them a chance to see how they could play out." She stood up, walked into the kitchen, and poured herself more coffee.

"There is the symbolic attack of the base itself. Bomb the gates, crash the fence, and fire shots from a boat."

"Fire shots from a boat? Why not a marine assault?"

"I looked at all the access points to the base. To get to Central Command or to Southern Command the only logical approaches are by land. A marine assault would require either a large vessel or many smaller vessels all of which would be identified early, and an easy defense response can be mounted. Air assaults are not practical with the closed airspace. A land assault could begin at the gates with no pre-warning due to all the civilian traffic off base."

Peter listened, thought a moment, and repeated his earlier thoughts, "What if the command staff and not the centers are the targets."

Sarah said, "I have played with it and it is plausible. The assault would have to be by water. Hit late at night or early morning when the staff is in their homes and a smaller tactical group could inflict damage. The command structures are reinforced and hard to reach except by vehicles and a ground assault. Inflict as much damage to personnel and you have a strong terror statement."

"So, what your saying is if personnel are the target, it will be a water assault and any smaller symbolic or building assaults will be through the gates." Peter asked.

"Command personnel. Yes water. And as I said before that is the way I would go but then again, I'm not a martyr. Martyrs are unpredictable."

Rafael speaks up. "Without information, the entire base, land, water, and air is a possibility. We are running on hunches and getting further assets in place will be difficult. I do believe we have every avenue covered as well as we can, especially once the HRT teams arrive to assist the marine units. I also spoke to the Coast Guard who will step up patrols around the base. I'll ask them to prioritize the evening hours."

Thinking out loud Peter asked, "You're right. Good call getting the Coast Guard involved. We have hardened as much as we can without specifics. What kind of armament do we have here in the house? Rafi and I can go through it all and itemize. Make sure we each have at least one M4, 10 full magazines, our handguns with extra magazines, bullet resistant vests, Kevlar helmets, first-aid kits, tactical flashlights, and night vision. We may want to go on shifts ourselves. Somethings coming. I'm with you Sarah, somethings coming."

Tomas logs into their email account and checks the drafts. A G-mail account was created so whenever they need to be careful in communications; log in, and check for drafts. If a message needs to be sent, type in the draft section and do not send. Therefore, the information cannot be intercepted. Anyone with the email information can log in and read the draft. Once the person it was intended for reads the draft, they delete it. This signals the drafter that the message was received.

There was a drafted email from Zarrin that read, "Hi T, Come on home Z." He deletes it and types another draft that said, "P, Let's go fishing soon. T." It was meant for Pedro, and Zarrin will notice hers is deleted and another typed. Tomas sends Pedro a text, "G" to indicate an email.

Pedro's phone sounds and he reads the text. He opens the computer, reads the draft from Tomas, and deletes it. Things were happening again.

"Anything yet?" Jose asked Tomas.

"Yes. We will go back to Tampa tomorrow."

The next day Tomas and Jose began their drive back. They travel to the mall at Westshore in Tampa and park in the parking lot with the thousands of shoppers. They walk to the entrance of an Italian restaurant and enter.

"How many and would you prefer a booth or a table?" The young girl behind the podium asks.

Tomas replies, "We are waiting for another."

"Take your time and let me know when you are ready."

They stand at the door for a little while and watch. They are still checking for surveillance after the events with Humberto and the appearance of the same people at the base. On the return drive, they stopped at a rest area and two exits to watch the cars that followed. At the rest area they sat in the picnic area watching for planes or drones. After 10 minutes, they return to the car and feel confident they were not followed. Guilty people always feel paranoid and Tomas knew this. Yet human nature dictates the paranoia because of the importance of the trip.

Tomas tells the girl at the desk they had a change in plans and were leaving. They walk back to the car, drive up the street to the Marriott hotel, and park in the self-parking lot. They remove their bags and call a cab. The cab picks them up and drives to the Tampa Shrimp docks. They pay and walk inside. Tomas had texted Pedro once they were in the car and he was waiting for them to arrive. It is dark and he gets them past the front gate. Walking out to the boat one of the other Captains see him with the other two in trail and asks, "Your crew?"

They all look up and Pedro smiles and waves at the man and said, "Yep. Gotta crew. Won't be around much longer. You ever find yours?"

"Nope. Waiting on a cousin to arrive to try and fill in."

"Keeping reliable people is always the hardest part of the job."

The other Captain looked down and waved. They walked onboard the *Mary Beth*.

"Something I need to know about?" Tomas asked Pedro.

"I will explain later. No worries. I have several good ideas to tell you. Wanna eat? Jose, go to the icebox below and see if anything appeals to you."

Jose said nothing, turns and walks away. After he was out of the room Pedro turns to Tomas and says, "That is part of what I have to tell you. The crew from the other boat I was discussing outside got nosey and I had to put them on ice."

Tomas straightens with a concerned look.

Seeing it, Pedro explains. "Nobody saw anything. These crews come and leave all the time. Happened a couple of days ago. All is still ready. We may be able to use them in our plan which is what I want to discuss with you." Smiling he said. "Jose should be back in a second."

As he finished the sentence, Jose came back in the room.

"What the hell Pedro?"

"Did they startle you?" Laughing.

"It's alright, Pedro told me about them. They will fit in our plan."

"Are they holding well?" Pedro asked with a smile.

"Frozen."

They all gathered in the lower cabin to bring each other up to date. It has been a while since the team had this time together. Pedro brings in coffee and boiled shrimp he prepared. They had much to discuss as the final plans are coming together. Pedro shows them the maps and the available places to stop and unload.

"Show me the maps of the base. Our friends gave me the locations of the command centers and housing." Tomas said.

Pedro pulls out the map and went to the floor next to the wall of the boat. He places the edge of a knife in the seam of the bottom molding and pulls it off. Behind this was a camera with no lens.

"It is too big with the telescopic lens attached so I keep the camera body here."

Turning it on he shows Tomas and Jose photos on the camera view screen to match the locations on the map. Jose has already surveilled and baselined the activity at the main gate to the base. With the collection of information, Tomas sips his coffee and thinks a moment. He looks over the maps and says, "This section of homes along the coast are the homes of the bosses and special guest."

"I can see with our number limitations that most operations will be symbolic and suicidal. I know each of you are willing to lay your lives down for the cause as am I. Sometimes, I like the way our enemies think when they say, 'Let the enemy die for their country, we will live for ours.' I did not prepare for this day for a symbolic demonstration. I have prepared to strike fear and respect into the minds of our enemies. We are going to assault the base but with a different plan. Ever since I was told of the target, I have been thinking of our options. There is no way we can overcome the base. The attempt is futile based on the reports everyone has given. What is possible is a large diversion and a coordinated attack at the weakest point. Go in by water and kidnap or kill their boss. The target is the Commandant of the base. The head of Central Command and the chief shot caller in the Middle East. The head of the snake. We will get to the General and take him out alive if possible and kill him if not.

His home is one of these." Pointing at the photographs of the large houses facing the water.

"We will find out and confirm which house is his." Jose said and Pedro smiles and nods.

"Find out. We will need distractions and I want them to pull away as many people as possible. We will have to move fast."

"What will we do with him once we have him?" Pedro asked.

"Yes, all contingencies have to be accounted for." Tomas replied as he scanned over the maps. He spread another map and then another of the State of Florida.

"I have been looking over different options since deciding on the plan. What is

this area?"

"The Ten Thousand Islands." Pedro answered.

"I like the name. They look like there are thousands of islands. I don't see many towns around there?"

"There aren't. You have Naples to the north, there." Pedro said and pointing to the map. "And Everglades City here on the inside of them. To the south there is nothing until you get to the Florida Keys."

"I like that." Tomas said.

"Look how far away it is from the base!" Jose proclaims.

"Yes, it is not an easy trip by boat. Slow and time for the Americans to catch us on this boat." Pedro said.

"Then we will not use this boat." says Tomas. "We will take their Commandant alive from his home to the Everglades and hold him there until things slow down. Then we can move him out of the country. Our secondary location can be here, near this town of Cedar Key to the north of the base. It too looks secluded."

"But Tomas, I can only imagine the numbers of people the Americans will use to search for the man." Jose said.

"Yes, they will, and they will expect certain transportation modes over others. We will choose the others." Looking at the two men. When they said nothing, he continued. "By car. If we move fast enough, they will not be capable of setting up to look for him and we will already be out of the area. They will expect boats or planes so we will go by car."

"Why are we taking him and not just killing him?" Jose asks.

"The effect and damage will last longer. If they move faster than we expect, then we will kill him and let them try to find the body."

"The Everglades are famous for their alligators." Pedro said and smiles saying nothing else. The reason was clear.

"Before anyone asks," Tomas says, "I have been given control over the operation to conduct as I see fit. I will let others that need to know of our intentions."

Pedro and Jose nodded their understanding.

Tomas is speaking his thoughts to show his control. He knows that for the many idiots above him, blame falls to the leader.

"Jose, I need you to rent a car and go to this Everglades City. If it is as appealing as it looks, rent a place for three months. I will give you cash to do this with. Make sure you use Enterprise because they will rent the car for cash. Make sure the location has direct water access."

He moves away to the other room and brings out a suitcase and gives Jose $7000.00.

"Let me know when you are done."

Jose nods and moves out of the cabin. He walks up to the end of the pier and uses a payphone to call a cab. There are few payphones left except in the areas with transient people like boat crews, bus stations, and such.

"Pedro mi amigo."

"Si jefe." You have performed flawlessly. I knew you would. That is why I wanted you all along."

"Thank you, jefe."

"No, please, call me Tomas. No more chain of command titles. In fact, while we are on the boat and around others, you will be jefe. The captain."

Pedro smiled, "Si Tomas. Understood."

"Ok. Let's look at the map you made and show me six locations at various points both above and below the base. I see that the exit to Tampa Bay runs to the south and west. This is the way they will expect us to travel. Did you also explore on this side?"

Pointing to the west is Pinellas County and the city of St. Petersburg.

"Si, yes. I have one concern. If we want to travel south by car towards the Everglades from here, we must go over the Sunshine Skyway. This is easy to shut down because there is nowhere to go with water on both sides."

"That makes sense. Ok let's look again here (pointing at the map) on the Tampa side south. We will have to plan how to remove him and transfer to another boat. This boat is slow and if we could transfer him to another sport vessel, it will blend in with the others."

"I agree." Pedro said. "We may want to look at a Friday, Saturday, or Sunday time. There are hundreds of recreational boats out here during the weekends."

"Agreed. Our target will be home then."

"Let me show you our best option for a boat ramp."

# 44

Jose caught a cab to the airport Enterprise rental car office. It takes a few moments, but they are convinced to rent a car for cash with a large down payment. He drives south on I-275 through Pinellas County and over the Sunshine Skyway bridge. Connecting to I-75 he makes the 2-hour drive to Alligator Alley. Paying the toll, he drives to the next exit, Highway 29 south. He stops at the small corner store at US41 and fills his gas tank in case he needs to return in a hurry. He arrives in Everglades City moments later. Staying on Copeland Drive he finds the Captains Table Lodge. Renting a room and texting Tomas, he settles in for the evening to look for properties in the morning.

Tomas places a message in the draft file intended for Zarrin. "I have seen the options and made a choice. Closing will be soon. Days even."

In the morning he sees a draft in the account.

"AA," it read. His message had been sent and the return message was short for "Allahu Akbar."

Waking early the next day, Jose looks in the newspaper for rental properties that matches their needs. He drives out Plantation Parkway to look at the first property. Arriving he knows it was too much and leaves. Driving back into town he sees trailers raised on concrete blocks to avoid the flood waters that often pass through the area. He finds a raised trailer in a cleaned-out area from the last hurricane off Copeland Avenue near the Ernest Hamilton Observation Tower.

"Perfect." He says to himself.

He calls the number on the sign and the owner agree to a 3-month furnished rental for $2000.00 per month, cash up front. The location is made. Time to return to Tampa. Four hours later he arrives at Tampa International Airport and turns in the car. He Uber's back to the boat.

"Jose, how was your trip?" Tomas inquired.

"Good. I have a place on the water. There are boat launches everywhere and few people around. Many of the businesses are being rebuilt after the last hurricane."

"Our plans are in place. We will soon be busy. Today is Tuesday. Rest today. I have plans for you and Pedro tomorrow."

Waking in the morning, Tomas instructs Pedro and Jose to buy two Toyota Corolla's for under $10,000.00 total.

"Make one beige and the other white if you can. I read online these are the most popular car colors in Florida. Can you believe that over one third of the people drive these cars and colors?"

Not saying anything Pedro nodded his head and waited as Jose pours another cup of coffee. Tomas brought out the cash.

"Seems like a lot of money. Why two cars?" Jose asked.

"Back up in case of problems."

Pedro and Tomas took the money and left. Tomas has time alone to review maps, the plans, routes and alternate routes. He leaves an email draft for Zarrin. In Orlando, Zarrin reads the draft and made plans to leave with her entourage. Flight plans are filed to complete in Paris. From there she can travel to Iran with ease. She has decided that whatever the plans are, she can show she was not in the United States when it starts. The FAA may close the airports depending on the severity of the plans. She will leave a team of ten to help Tomas as well as a used 24-foot Wellcraft Cuddy Cabin boat as requested in the email draft. Several of the team members are women and Zarrin provides a medical kit with sedatives in the boat. They will be helpful in keeping the general under control.

Peter wakes the next morning and walks out for coffee. Rafael is on the phone and Sarah is in her room. Rafi looking at Peter stops and places his hand over the phone.

"She was up late working on more contingencies."

Peter nodded and Rafael returned to the phone call. When finished he looks at Peter who had sat at the kitchen table.

"That was Captain Sears. He has assigned an additional 4-man team to the General. He still has a few on the outside running surveillance. I hope we are planning this right. The QRF is still in place and all necessary supplies provided. The FBI-HRT and their black boats are in place at the base marina. Their mobile facilities are functioning, and they can react within minutes to any threat."

"Sounds good. Thanks. We are in a wait and see mode now." Peter responded.

Tomas says to Pedro. "Tell me more about Williams Park in Gibsonton."

"It is a big ramp next to a Phosphate plant. There is no security there but busy. Something I noticed is Mosaic Park with a tennis court on the other side of the road. It has a parking lot that no one uses. There is a concealed shoreline with easy access from the water near the railroad tracks. From there a car can go south a half mile and east on Gibsonton Drive connecting with I75 or east to US 301. North or south from there. Starting at the edge of the base to the mouth of the river is 4 miles and another mile up the river, under the US41 bridge and Mosaic Park will be on the left." Pedro describes as he's pointing out all of the locations.

"I like it."

"Do you know what our plans are?"

"I'm getting close. We will meet for final planning soon."

Tomas places a message in the email draft folder Thursday night. Amir and Hamid were placed in charge of the team left by Zarrin. They opened the draft and read it together. "Meet me at Sonny's BBQ on Dale Mabry Friday at 2:30 PM."

They erased the message telling Tomas it was received. Friday afternoon, they made arrangements to be at the restaurant and met with Tomas and Pedro.

"Hello!" Tomas said as the two approached the table.

Pedro stood and they all hugged and shook hands.

"Please, have a seat. Tell me what is new." Tomas said.

Pedro moved to Tomas' side of the table and sat on the inside. Tomas was not going to feel trapped on the inside of the table and wants to face the entrance to see who enters after Amir and Hamid. The time was chosen between typical dining hours and few were there. He selected a table in the back of the restaurant underneath a ceiling speaker playing country music. The music seamed louder than normal because there was no one else creating background noise.

After brief small talk, Tomas saw no one else enter the restaurant. He looked at the others and started discussing the plans. He pointed at a map he had spread on the table. He looks up and sees a waitress walking towards them and he held up his hand to tell her to stop, smiling he says, "We are alright for now. We have business to discuss. Can I get your attention later to assist us?"

"Yes sir. Of course, you can. Y'all let me know if there is anything you need." She turned and walked back to the front of the restaurant.

Tomas returns to the map. "We have conducted surveillance on the land entrances and water around the base. Let me tell you what I need from you."

They all lean in closer and listen. An hour later they rise up from their table. Amir and Hamid left the meeting and met with their teams. The plan was set for Sunday morning. The day after tomorrow. There is only one day to organize. Amir's team will be part of the marine assault and Hamid will attack by land. Most operations need more time. This plan is so precise that extra time is unnecessary and the longer it is strung out, the greater the likelihood of a mistake.

Hamid selects Davoud for the main gate operation and shows him location targets and the equipment he needs. He selects another man to go with him. The other two will stay with Hamid for another operation.

Amir met with his team to discuss the plans. They have more to prepare. He tells the females, Yasmin and Esther to go shopping and gave them a list. He tells the other men to prepare the boat with fuel and weapons. He looks over the maps and equipment list.

# 45

Sunday morning, no one slept. Davoud and his partner Javier leave early and drive to Brandon. They arrive before anyone else at the public transportation lot. This is designated as a bus pick up for defense contractors that takes them to MacDill AFB. It picks up passengers at 5:00 AM each morning and they travel through Tampa to the front gate of the base. It is still dark when the bus arrives and there are not as many riders on the weekend. As they board, Davoud steps out and walks up to the rear of the bus. He looks back and Javier gave him a thumbs up and he laid on the ground. He places the bomb up in the engine housing and walks back and gets in the car. They said nothing as they follow the bus onto the empty street. Forty minutes later they are at the front gate of the base. Davoud and Javier stop in the parking lot of a bank as they watch the bus pull up to the right visitor's lane and stop.

Hamid and his team load their weapons and drive to a position near the Bayshore Ave entrance to MacDill. Javier is to text him to know when to start the second attack. Hamid will hesitate a moment to see if any of the guards at the Bayshore gate leave before beginning their assault. He and his men readied their weapons and move within a block of the second base gate.

Amir and his team of men and women arrive at Williams Park towing their Wellcraft boat. They launch into the Alafia River after buying a parking pass for the day. No reason to take chances in case they return from the mission. It is a minor concern to not get caught for failure to pay a $5.00 fee. They park the car and trailer halfway up the driveway. They know many people will arrive as the morning progresses and their car and trailer will be in the middle with no attention drawn to it. The first arrivals park closer to the ramp so they can leave easier. It will look like their car was parked hours after others. The parking pass is on the dash not to draw undue attention.

Tomas, Jose, and Pedro board the shrimp boat and leave early. They travel using GPS to the edge of a spoil island at the mouth of the Alafia River. Spoil islands are created during dredging projects to open channels for shipping. The sand is dredged and dumped in an area that creates an island. They wait to meet with Amir and his team. Tomas and Jose are scanning the base shoreline, now about 2 miles away, and the waters between. About 4:30 AM they hear a boat approaching from the river and they turn their attention to it. It's Amir and his team. They pull up to the shrimp boat and Tomas looks over their crew.

"Hello Amir. All is well?"

"Yes Tomas. We are ready."

"This is Yasmin and Esther. Do you approve of their suits?"

"Yasmin and Esther, you did find the most revealing of swimsuits."

They smiled, and it was obvious they were not comfortable wearing string and cloth patches as bathing suits.

Tomas recognized Esther as the girl he first met in the parking lot of the hotel when he was told to go to the Brandon mall to meet Zarrin.

"Jose and I will go in with you. Pedro will move closer in case we need help."

"Pedro," Tomas said, "get rid of the cargo you have on ice. We no longer need them. It is up to Hamid to start."

Pedro nodded and said, "I can leave them on the boat's deck after I escape to confuse the investigators as to why these guys were involved in the attack."

Tomas nodded and said, "Good idea."

Speaking to everyone Tomas said, "We will wait until we see the attack has started before going to the base."

He then sent a text to Javier that everyone was ready. Tomas and Jose board the boat and they move east towards the shoreline. Pedro went below to drag the bodies of the shrimpers to the deck. He needs them to start thawing out. He moved back to the boat bridge and continued slow towards the shore and watching through binoculars. He moved several weapons including 2 AK47's he was given, next to him.

Tomas is low and watching for the presence of a police boat. At one mile from the base shoreline, they slow. At less than a half mile away, police blue lights came on not from one, but 2 boats. The plans were in place and the men move below into the cuddy cabin. Only Yasmin and Esther are visible. The first boat pulls up to the right side of the Wellcraft. There are two state officers on board and one of them laid out their side bumpers.

"Good morning, ladies. This is a restricted area. You are not allowed here." Both officers smiling and scanning the two women up and down.

"Were sorry officer. We are trying to be the first at our favorite beach for a party today, but there seems to be something wrong with the boat. Thank goodness you men are here. Can you take a look? Please?"

The officers smiled at each other and all safety protocols left as they board the boat. The second police boat arrives and it is part of the military police from the base with a single officer on board.

As the marine officers board the boat, Yasmin said, "I think part of the problem is the wires down there." Pointing into the cabin of the boat. Ester steps to the edge and captures the attention of the young Air Policeman.

"Hello!" She said.

The young man steps away from his boat console and said, "Hello to you. Are you alright?"

"We are now." Ester replies with a grin as she leans to her left and lifts a silenced pistol.

As the two boarding officers move forward to look for wiring, Amir and 2 other men reach out of the cabin and grab them. Tomas steps out of the cabin to see if more help is needed. The officers were stabbed multiple times by several men waiting in ambush. Tomas said nothing as he came out of the cabin, turning towards the second police boat and sees Yasmine leaping onto the second boat with Ester. The young officer was shot in the chest which knocks him back onto the deck. He tries in desperation to reach his radio, but Ester is already on his boat and approaching. She fires another shot that strikes him in his arm and then another woman appears. Yasmin sat next to him and smiles and says, "It will be alright." Her voice is so calming it made him pause a moment. She brought the knife around and his life drains as she stares, smiling into his eyes.

"What do we do with the bodies?" Amir asked.

"Take off the tops of their uniforms and throw the bodies overboard. We are no longer concerned about attention."

"This is better than I had planned." Tomas said under his breath.

With the women and Jose wearing the top halves of the uniforms, they collect the weapons and ammo from the boats. Tomas tells Yasmin and Esther to take both police boats and move south and watch the marina.

"We should soon see the fireworks created by the others at the gates. When this happens, move in and kill. Everybody is a target. Stay in this area to protect our escape in case there are other boats in the marina."

# 46

Davoud and Javier watch the bus approaching the front gate of the base. The air police approach the bus and board to check the ID of the passengers. Javier sends a text to Hamid signaling the attack will be soon. With the police on board, Davoud detonates the explosives. The blast is large and fiery and lifts the back of the bus off the ground. Afterwards, he drives to the gates and jumps out and shoots another officer who was knocked down by the blast and trying to stand up in the gate house. A Humvee races in and they begin exchanging gunfire with the airmen inside.

A moment later, Hamid drives through the other gate and begins shooting at several soldiers occupying another Humvee. They drive past the military vehicles and drive in the direction of the Central Command building.

An alarm sounds in the hanger housing the QRF team and they load the vehicles and begin to move out. The resting team begins dressing to get into action behind the first team.

"Where is it." Captain Sears says after he answers his phone. "Both gates?" as he listens a moment. "One of them has broken past? What about the QRF? Good keep them updated. Wait a minute! Put a call to Peter Berk and his team at the Weller home and alert the base commander."

A large explosion is seen to the north as well as the distinct clatter of gunfire. The two police boats with Yasmin and Esther approach another boat with their blue lights on at the entrance to the marina. As they slow, the two military officer's inside are on the radio and looking to the north. As they pull up to them the others yelled, "What the hell is going…" And before they could finish the sentence, they are shot dead with automatic weapons fire.

Yasmin yells over, "Esther, move inside of the marina by the docks. I will move closer to cover you but also stay out to watch for other approaching boats."

Esther accelerates towards the marina. Yasmin follows a short distance and stops. As Esther arrives in the marina, she sees two large black boats with seats in the front and inflatable siding. She stops with her blue lights on. Within seconds, several men came out of a group of motor homes and ran down to board the boats. She moves closer and began shooting at them. The first jumps into the HRT boat and the second jumps off the dock into the water on the opposite side. More men are running from the motor homes and Esther fires on them. From outside the marina, Yasmin hears the gunfire and looks around for any other boats. Seeing none, she moves closer to the marina.

With all the activity started, Tomas has already reached the shoreline and all five men jump out. They move up the bank to a small wall used as a water barrier. They cross the road and stop at the wall in front of General Burns' home.

"Jose." Tomas says. "Stay here out of sight and provide cover if we need it. When you see us running back, go to the boat and start the engines to prepare for our escape."

The lights came on in the Commanders home and Tomas turned and approached. The lights to the north of the commander's home came on a moment later.

Asleep in bed, there was a knock on his bedroom door, and it opens. Sarah is there. "Peter, I was up working on the computer and thought I heard an explosion."

"Let me get dressed. Go outside and verify if it sounds like anything and if so wake up Rafi. My phone hasn't rung."

Sarah went out the back door where sound is heard better without the bay washing ashore. In the distance to the north, she hears the distinct sound of gunfire. She turns to go in and then heard gunfire to the southwest from the marina.

Running in she is yelling, "It's started." She runs towards Rafi's room.

Peter's phone rang and vibrated, and he answered. "This is base communications. Captain Sears told me to call you that the front gates are under attack."

"Has General Burns and other staff been notified?"

"Yes sir. Just before you."

"Ok. Call in help from civilian police."

Peter hangs up and got dressed. He moves to the living room where Sarah is laying out their equipment and weapons. Rafi comes out in shorts and slips on shoes and throws on a vest, charges his M4 and moves towards the back door. Peter moves to the front and Sarah followed Rafi out the back.

She yells, "Gunfire to the north and from the direction of the marina."

"Roger that. Watch out. There are extra security officers around the house. Don't get killed by friendlies." Peter yells out hoping Rafi heard him.

Peter moves out the front of the house, Rafi and Sarah out the back. They all move south towards General Burns home.

Davoud and Javier separate and take up positions to fire on any approaching cars. Hamid and his car drive down the road, cross several fields and see four Humvees approaching. It is the first QRF team.

"Drive straight at them." Hamid yells from the rear of the car. "You must crash into them."

The driver looks back and again forward.

"Javad." He calls to the front passenger. Jump out and we will continue the fight. The driver slows and Hamid and Javad open their doors and fall out of the car. The driver floors the accelerator.

As the four Humvees approach, they spread out.

"What the hell is he doing?" The driver of the front Humvee yells out.

"Watch out he's not slowing down!" Another yelled.

Hamid's driver slows his speed for more control and as he approaches the Humvee the distance is closing too fast and he manages to scream out "Allahu!" before impact. Though the Humvee is heavier the velocity and angle of the impact along with no one in the Humvee wearing a seatbelt; the collision is thunderous. Bodies of the team members in the rear of the truck fly into the air. Those inside are thrown through the front windshield. There is no fire from these types of crashes, just smoke.

From inside one of the other Humvees the order to stop is given. They pull up in shock of what they have seen. Then from the dark field ahead of them they take gunfire.

"QRF 2 this is QRF 1 over! QRF 2 this is QRF 1 can you read me."

"QRF 1 this is QRF 2. Go ahead."

"We have lost a truck and have casualties. We are under small arms fire half mile in from the south gate. Over."

"Roger that. Do you need us there?"

"Negative. Go to the main gate."

"Roger. Main gate."

Another Humvee arrives at the main gate and is silhouetted by the flames of the exploded bus. Davoud and Javier are exchanging gunfire with the security personnel. From the City of Tampa, police officers are arriving at both gates and notifying dispatch of the attack and requesting backup. From the south gate, police officers move past the gate and into the base itself. In the distance they hear gunfire.

Tomas and one of Amir's men move closer to the front of the house on the south side as Amir and the other man move to the north. Approaching the house an armed man steps out from behind a column and yells "Stop or I'll shoot!" Tomas sights him and pulls the trigger. He goes down. More lights are coming on in the house as the General's family awakens.

Tomas looks at the other man and says, "We have to get in quick."

They raise up and move towards a set of French doors. Tomas sends a blast of rounds to the center latch as the other man rushes and slams through the door. As he does, another armed officer opens fire on the man as he rolls over the floor. Tomas enters and fires on the security officer and he goes down. He looks at his man. He is shot in the leg and is trying to tie off the bleeding. The wounded man looks up at Tomas and says, "Go on. I'm ok. I'll catch up and cover."

Tomas nods and moves on.

On the north side of the home Amir and his man move up to the corner of the porch and engage a security officer. After taking him out, another burst of gunfire hit the wall coming from their north. Rafi moves to the separation wall between the properties and sees the two men moving and shoot the security officer. He engages them. Peter is moving south towards the front of the house and hears the gunfire.

"Stay here and keep them away." Amir said to his man. Amir continues to move to the rear of the house.

At the marina, Esther takes more fire until one shot hits its target. Yasmin, driving into the marina sees her go down. The HRT team advances to the dock unaware that Yasmin driving the security police boat, is the enemy. The driver of the boat who jumped off the dock is climbing onto the boat from the water with the dock to his back. Without hesitation, Yasmin slams the throttle full forward and the boat lifts as it reaches plane. She steers the boat toward the rear of the first boat, braces herself as it strikes the left side and rear, goes airborne, and comes down on top of the second. The agent climbing out of the water sees the action taken too late and is crushed between the boats. Other agents rush the boat and Yasmin is killed. Both FBI boats are out of action.

As the QRF 2 team approaches the front gate, Davoud places a few shots into their lead car. Javier is engaging the civilian police behind and is struck. He tries to continue the fight, but another officer has flanked his position and shoots him dead.

Hamid and Javad continue to fire and hold down the QRF 1 team until they see the police cars approaching from behind.

"Don't stop behind them! We will be in their cross-fire!" One of the officer's yells into his microphone. "Go left! Go left!"

The police cars drive left and place Hamid and Javad in a L-shaped kill zone. They are both killed moments later.

Overwhelmed and wounded, Davoud running low on ammunition stands and charges the QRF 2 team and is killed.

"QRF 1 this is QRF 2 over."

"QRF 1 go ahead."

"We are secure with the local police at the main gate."

"Same here at the south gate. We have casualties."

"QRF 1 stay and attend to your wounded. We are moving to the marina. Another attack there on the FBI teams."

"Roger that."

The QRF 2 team left one vehicle at the gate and started their drive to the opposite end of the base when another call comes in.

"QRF 1 and 2, General Burns home is under attack!"

# 47

Tomas slowly enters the kitchen. There he sees General Burns and his wife with a security officer. He fires from the shadow and drops the officer and General Burns holds up a pistol and fires as his wife screams. Tomas fires and strikes the General in the right shoulder and he drops the pistol.

"Come with me General."

"Fuck you!"

Tomas turned the barrel of his rifle and shoots his wife through the head. Blood and brain matter flies across the kitchen and splashes across the General.

"Come with me. Now!"

From the living room they hear the family's son Jason, "Dad! Mom! Where are you? What's going on?"

Stunned by the sight and the need to protect his son, the General leaps for the pistol while yelling, "Run Jason!"

Tomas fires again striking the General in the stomach. The door fly's open and Tomas fires on Jason, the bullets throwing the boy's body into the other room. He turns back to the General and shoots him in the head.

Rafi and Amir's partner continue to exchange fire. Sarah moves right towards the sound of the gunfire knowing it is coming from where she last saw Rafi. Peter moves to the front of the house scanning the area. He sees the downed security officer and the broken door and enters. His peripheral vision is nonexistent due to the stress of the scene. He knows he must pause and continue to scan if he intends to see any threats not in front.

People watch videos of special operations forces as they move through their scenes. They wonder why not move fast to rescue victims. Under stress we lose our peripheral vision zones locking into center gaze focus known as tunnel vision. Our eyes lose depth perception and we become far sighted. We lose fine muscle movements and eye hand coordination. Movements and heartrate have to be controlled. Operators learn to shoot without sights by creating muscle memory movements to bring their weapons on target to the front.

Peter continues his slow movements toward the center of the rear of the house. Rafi moves to change his angle and sees someone to his left. The attacker sees the movement as well during this lull and fires. Rafi raises from his new angle and sights in the attacker and drops him. He jumps the wall and moves left to the other figure who is down.

"Sarah!" Rafi yells.

He reaches her and allows his training to take over as he sweeps her body for wounds. Sarah, panting and eyes wide open tries to speak.

"It's alright Sarah. I'm going to get you out of here."

He pulls her vest and her shirt is covered in blood. The wound is side to side. He knows there is no saving her but tries to pack the wounds.

Peter moves through the house. In the living room he sees Jason's body. He eases into the kitchen and sees the bodies and moves past. No time for grief and shock. Moving back into the living room he sweeps left and right. A door opens and Peter double taps the man twice in the head. Amir falls dead.

Tomas exits the house and runs across the lawn. Jose seeing him turns and crosses the road back to the boat and starts the engine. Tomas clears the wall and sees Humvees driving towards him from the north and he sprints across the street and leaps onto the rear of the boat. Jose accelerates but the water is too shallow and the engine skeg hits the bottom and the prop digs in. He slows the engine speed. They have to move slow a little longer. Tomas looks back and sees the wounded man he entered the house with step into the street and fire on the Humvees.

Peter exits the front of the house and sees a man jump the wall. He sprints in his direction. Seeing another man firing at the QRF team, Peter drops him dead with a 3-round burst. The QRF arrives and sees a man running from the front of the house and a boat trying to move to their left as they are taking fire from a man in the road. He goes down as Peter yells "Stop the boat! Stop the boat! They killed the General!"

"Drop your weapon!" They yelled back.

Looking at the boat the QRF team members see it is not a police boat and the order is given, "Shoot the boat!"

They opened fire as it gains speed. A man at the rear is firing back. Another larger boat is approaching from the north.

With rounds striking around them, Jose yells, "Look! it's Pedro. I'll move towards him."

Pedro's only order was support if he saw it was needed. After the others left to start the mission, he moved closer to watch the activities on shore and assist where needed. He saw the firefight in front of the home the explosions to the north at the gates and more gunfire and a loud crash to the south by the marina. He accelerated the shrimp boat and moved to the north. As he watched the boat pull away from shore a group of Humvees pulled up and opened fire. Running south parallel to the shore he raised an AK and opened fired on the convoy. His aim more effective than Tomas' with the stable platform of the shrimp boat and not the bouncing Wellcraft. Tomas and Jose slip to the left and are now blocked by the shrimp boat that is receiving all the gunfire from shore.

"Want me to go back for Pedro?"

"No." Tomas yelled "Get in the river and to the park as fast as you can."

Tomas looked back at Pedro who had moved to the left side of the boat to see what they were going to do. He watches as the boat disappears now knowing they will not pick him up. He is on his own.

Two U.S. Coastguard 25-foot Defender Class boats are approaching from the south and engage the shrimp boat with 50-calber machine guns mounted on the bow. These are too heavy for the shrimp boat to endure and moments later the boat is dead in the water. Its Captain torn almost in half after being hit by several of the rounds.

At the house Peter is on his cellphone and Rafi finally answers.

"Where the hell are you? Are you ok? Have you seen Sarah?"

"I'm fine. Sarah's dead. North side of Burns house."

Silence for a moment. "What? How? On my way."

"She was shot. I was able to put the guy down. Are you ok? Where are you? The                                                                                          General?"

"I'm alright. Generals dead. His family too. I'm moving towards you from the front of the house. A QRF is here and spreading out around the property. Don't know if any of them are left. Be on guard." He hung up.

Captain Sears races up with another OSI agent.

"Peter, are you alright?"

"Yeah. The general and his family are dead. Contact the Coast Guard. There is another boat out there moving due east from the shrimp boat."

Tomas and Jose enter the Alafia River. Two miles to go.

"Don't slow down Jose. We do not care about attention now. We have to get to the cars."

Jose nodded. They cruised past the Phosphate plant and the Williams Park boat ramps. The railroad bridge which is less than 10 feet above the water is open. There's enough light now to see and they cruise through the bridges and make a hard left throwing a wake onto a small fishing boat approaching the same bridge from the east. The men in the boat yell curse words and discuss a moment trying to follow 'the son-of-a bitch driving the boat' but decide instead to continue to their fishing spot.

Jose shuts down and raises the engine before the bow hits the shore.

"Hang on!" He yells.

Tomas grips the seat and the boat lunges to a stop. They both climb out and run to the cars in the parking lot.

"Both cars?" Jose asks.

"Yes. Follow me."

They each climb into a car and drive east on Riverview Drive. Down the road they stop at the Showmen's Museum parking lot and Tomas parks his car. He runs to the passenger's side and tells Jose to continue east to US301 and go south. "Get to I75 and go to Everglades City. Do not get pulled over for something stupid like speed. Keep moving and we will be out of their immediate watch area."

A few moments later, the fisherman get past the Phosphate plant when they see a U.S. Coast Guard boat moving fast into the river and slow near all the moored boats around Williams Park. Overhead police and Coast Guard helicopters are circling.

"You think their looking for those sons-of-bitches that almost ran into us?"

"Might be. I'll wave them over."

Minutes later, police vehicles are in Mosaic Park securing the scene. There is an abandoned boat and witnesses saw two men on board. An immediate area search is in place.

Peter arrives to Rafi. He is sitting near Sarah's body covered with his shirt. Peter kneeled and Rafi started talking without being asked. He needed to tell the story.

"She was moving along the inside of the wall and I was on the outside exchanging gunfire with a guy. There was a lull with the shooter, and I was changing positions. She did not know where anyone was and moved slow while scanning. I guess the shooter moved during the lull as well because he started shooting, not at me or where I was but my left further up the wall. I saw the movement and assumed it was Sarah and his muzzle flash exposed him, and I took him down. I jumped the wall, moved up and that's when I saw her body. She was spot on about how the attack would happen. Spot on."

Peter didn't say anything as he looked down and heard Rafi take a deep breath in and then out.

"Did we get everybody?"

"No." Peter said. "Some escaped on boat. The Coast Guard is after them."

Rafi stared at him without saying anything.

# 48

When you are in the business of life and death, the announcement of death is best accepted directly.

"John it's Peter. We have a real cluster here. Sarah's dead."

"Damnit!"

He knew the next question, so he answered. "She was shot and killed, General Burns and his family were all assassinated."

Silence on the other end for a few seconds. "Other casualties?"

"Still counting. They blew up a civilian bus with contractors going to the base that also killed some Air Force Security Police Forces. I know one of the QRF teams lost some, the FBI HRT team lost some as well as a few state marine officers are missing.

"It's all on me. It was on my watch. We had it pegged. They came in as Sarah predicted. Time and resources hurt us." John said.

"It's not on you. We were all in charge here. Sarah was right but we didn't know it at the time. We covered it the best we could. They succeeded. They won. Hindsight is always easier."

"They won a battle. We're on the offense now. I'll deal with the bullshit from here. You have a standing order. Kill these bastards. Find them wherever and by whatever means and kill them. No trial to expand their cause. Do not bring them in. Get intel on anyone attached if possible and kill them too. Do you understand me?"

"Yes." Peter said without hesitation. "I'll keep you up to date."

Hatfield hung up without responding.

Sarah, the Burns family and the casualties from the different scenes were taken to the base hospital. The best in the country were enroute to MacDill on orders of the President. With this many autopsies and identification processes to oversee, the more personnel the better.

A small car pulls up to a rental home in Everglades City after driving around for 30 minutes. Some saw the men drive past and thought nothing of it. They carried their bags inside.

"Set up the house, unpack the bags and close the blinds. Decide on the rooms and start some tea. Pack a Go-Bag for each of us with identification, clothes, and a weapon." Tomas told Jose.

"Ok. The refrigerator is stocked. I put food and drinks there when I was last here."

Tomas nodded and stepped to the back of the house and pulled out a burner unused Boost phone. He opened his computer and placed a message into the draft email and waited for the reply.

Peter was at Mosaic Park looking over the abandoned boat when his phone rang.

"Hey Peter, John. Anything new?"

"Yeah, we have another scene when the security guard called in to say there was an abandoned car at the Showmen's Museum down the street from the park. Crime scene technicians are there now. I'm going through the paperwork on this boat trying to discover something. There was a medical bag left on board with enough sedatives to knock out an elephant. My guess is in case they could kidnap the General; probably their first goal. There was a shrimp boat with a man. We believe a Mexican national on board that provided cover for the escaping boat. The captain and the boat were shredded by the Coast Guard when he fired on them."

Peter hesitated a moment and said, "There were three people dead on that shrimp boat. Two of them had been dead awhile. They were probably kept in the ice box of the boat and pulled to the deck the morning of the attack based on their level of thaw."

"So, they were probably crew or owners of the boat and killed for the boat."

"Don't know yet."

"What was the name of the boat?"

"Mary Beth. Coast Guard believes it may be a missing vessel from Texas."

"Ok. I've got the NSA redirecting resources to our people. We've been putting fingerprints and facial ID and any electronic footprints through their databases."

"Thanks. We'll keep info flow both ways."

Most people are unaware of the information collected by the NSA. They have tapped into the cables that connect mobile networks globally and cellphones both nationally and internationally. NSA analysts can use this information to find cellphones anywhere in the world. They then retrace the phones movements and find relationships among the people using them. It collects locations in bulk and the process is known as "Co-Traveler". This bulk information is analyzed to allow their system to look for other connections between known and unknown targets by tracking people whose movements connect by telephone. This system location data uses mathematical analogues to enable analysts to map cellphone owners' relationships by connecting their movements over time with thousands of other phone users who cross their paths. Cellphones broadcast their locations even when they are not being used.

This allows NSA to track people from business meetings, personal visits to anywhere from hotel rooms to private homes. It also demands the collection and storage of the data. Data this massive in volume needs sophisticated systems and storage processes. Bringing the links together takes time to sift through.

John called Peter again and said, "NSA has been tasked to cross-reference information from phones around the base at the time of the attack. Lucky for us, there were few people up and on their phones at the time."

"Good to hear. Anything yet?"

"Text and calls were made from phones outside the base, the Williams Park boat ramps, the Tampa Shrimp docks, and they are cross-referencing those to others. There may be some email traffic as well."

"Ok. I'll keep working things from here until I get another direction."

After hanging up, Peter told Rafi he was going to the Tampa Shrimp Docks.

"I'll go with you. Nothing to do here. Cameras are pulling up video of the people who bought the car."

They arrived at the docks and stopped by several of the boats to speak to the captains.

"How are you today. We are from Washington assisting on the base attack investigation. You mind if we ask you a few questions?" Peter asked.

"You think this place is connected to the base attack?"

"We believe someone here may have been involved."

"Normally I would say I do mind. We don't like talking to government people because it usually is something against us. 'We're from the government and here to help' is never the truth in commercial fishing. But the one thing we are is patriotic. Won't tolerate this crap against our country. What do you want to ask? If I can help I will."

"Glad to hear and understand your concerns. We are looking into a shrimp boat that was destroyed and wondering if it was from around here."

"Who's was it?"

"Looking into all that but the name was Mary Beth."

The captain looked at him and said, "The Mary Beth? Yeah, it's been here for a while. Maybe a month. Staying across there at the guest dock. A Hispanic guy running it. No crew until the other day when a couple more Hispanic guys showed up."

"Couple more? Can you describe them? Seen them before?"

"No never seen them. The captain, I think his name was Pedro or something was working on his boat every day and running sea trials. Said when all was shipshape, he was going to the Keys."

"Anybody missing around here?"

"Missing? Don't know about missing but a couple of my guys took off. That's why I'm still here. Can't go out without a full crew."

"What were their names?"

"Daniel Reeves and Charles Johnson. We called them Danny and Chuck. Why do you ask about them? They ain't the smartest hands I ever had but they ain't terrorist."

"Thanks for all your help. Someone else may be in touch."

After getting back into their car, Peter called John.

"That boat was over here at the Tampa Shrimp docks. Said it was captained by a Hispanic guy who had a couple of other guys show up the other day to work with him."

"You think those are the two on ice?"

"No, the captain I was talking to was across from where the boat was docked and he's missing two crew members. I'd bet on them."

"Maybe. There's more information about that shrimp boat. It's out of Corpus Christi and went missing. Never returned from a shrimping trip. Crew of three. Coast Guard searched for a while but gave up. Placed word throughout the Gulf Coast to be on the lookout."

"Who was the captain?"

"The owner is a man named Kurt Johnson. It was captained by Pedro Gomez. There was another man on board."

"Pedro is the same name we received here from the other boat captain and the office."

"I'm working on it. We'll turn that body over to the FBI. I'll get pictures of the guys on ice and have locals go by the docks there to make ID."

"Sounds good." Peter said. "Anything else from cell phones?"

"Yeah. From all over the area we are cross referencing them. Already linking them to phones found at the scenes. They are working around the clock in shifts to cross them to any other phone and person."

"Anything unusual standing out? Number of calls or people that don't fit in?" Peter's US Marshall fugitive task force mind is working on angles.

"Yeah. Tracking them to restaurants and each other. Not too many strangers or friends outside of the link."

"How many out of the area?"

"A few from the St Augustine area, Orlando, and many throughout Brandon."

"Brandon fits with all the other events over the past few months. When were the Orlando, St Augustine events?"

"The weeks before the attack. Right after the woman jihadi was killed in the police standoff."

Thinking to himself Peter knew they had left the area to allow things to cool down. Then he asked, "Anything else?"

"There was a couple of numbers in contact but ended the day before. They may have returned in Iran."

"There's a strong connection."

"There was a single text out of Everglades City."

"When?"

"Couple of days ago."

"Did that number show up before?"

"Yes. Been in the area a while."

"Alright. Why all the way down there just before? That's where I want to go."

"Go. Take what you need. Remember, nothing has changed."

"Roger that." Peter hung up and knew what was meant. Kill them.

"Rafi." Peter called over. "You alright?"

"Yeah, but I need to tie up a few loose ends. Anything up?"

"No. Nothing new. I'll let you know."

"Ok. Roger that."

Peter could see the effect of Sarah's death on him. He too felt the inner pain of loss. But the rest of the team had worked longer together, and his heart and mind had no room for pain. He was set to seek and destroy.

Peter returned to the Weller house on base and put together a bag. He packed a Glock 27 .40 cal for a bigger punch and concealment abilities compared to the popular 9mm, a S&W model 60 .38 with +P ammo, and an M4. He carried extra magazines for each and speed loaders for the revolver. People always ask, "Why a revolver?" The answer is easy. "They never fail." He also packed night vision, 100% Deet bug repellent, changes of clothes including a bug jacket since he was going to the Everglades. The Deet will work but has an odor. He may need to go close and any change in the wind could give him away. Last, he packed two knives. One straight blade K-Bar and a folding Emerson. Knives are for defensive and quiet offensive tactics. A man skilled with a knife is another's worst nightmare. He is deadlier and stealthier with a good knife and a skill set. In the garage he sees several fishing rods and reels. He gathered them thinking what Everglades City is known for; fishing. If he was going to snoop around, he had better look like he belongs. He returned to the master bedroom and looked in the closet. He found some Skinny Matters fishing shirts and hats he could use to blend into the fishing environment. It is a brand that specializes in sun shirts for shallow water fishing and that is what the Everglades are famous for.

He loads a van and left the base. Thirty minutes later and he is southbound on I75. Two hours later he passes through Fort Myers, then Naples and exits before the toll booth for Alligator Alley to avoid the toll plaza camera system. He instead takes Tamiami Trail stopping to top off the gas tank before calling it a night at Contys Motel about 30 miles from Everglades City. He doesn't know what he's about to encounter and doesn't want his face seen often around town.

Rising early the next day he showers and finishes it off with a cold blast of water to wake up. He makes some coffee and drinks it down and fills a to go cup. Everglades City is a small town and even fewer people in the heat of summer. Looking over the map he thinks of the areas he would look for if he wanted to hide. Many say to hide in plain sight amongst the populous, so you blend in better. However, scared and nervous people see the boogie man at every corner and will find an out of the way location. He calls Hatfield via a secure satellite phone for an update.

John tells him, "We are working on the angles. The car they found abandoned was matched by tire tracks to the tracks at the park where the boat was abandoned. The other tracks are of the same type of car. A small car. A Corolla was found abandoned so something like that."

"Ok. Send me a message if anything critical comes in and I'll check back with you."

"Let me know if you need anything." John replies.

Tomas places the email message with the contact information for the burner phone. Opening the email, Zarrin reads the message and then deletes it. She responds, "Congratulations on the success of your game. The whole family is very proud. We need to get together soon and celebrate. Tell us where you want to meet."

Tomas smiles and looks up at Jose, "We did well my friend. They all know it and are proud."

Smiling Jose says, "What's our plan now? Are they coming for us?"

Tomas thinking a moment looks up at Jose and says, "Soon. We must stay low for a while."

He types, "Everglades City."

"Where are they?" Zarrin asks her assistants having never left the United States.

"We are locked in on Everglades City."

"Good. They still trust us to help. Put it together and let's go now. No loose ends."

Peter decides to begin in the Chocoloskee area which is at the bottom of Copeland Ave where it turns into Smallwood Drive. All he has are people he believes are Hispanic or Persian and a small car. He looks at restaurants and drives around looking at residences. Within a couple of hours, he has looked at all the homes and moves north along Copeland Ave. He sees areas on both sides cleaned out by the latest hurricane that devastated the area. He notices driving north there is new construction made of high-rise trailers to help the next flood waters sweep beneath instead of away. He passes the Ernest Hamilton Observation Tower and a marina and turns right into one of the areas being cleaned up. He notices that everyone here drives either a truck or an SUV. This is to pull your boat because outside of boating there is little to do. He looks left and right and on the back side of a high-rise trailer he sees an older Toyota Corolla with a temporary paper Florida tag. He memorizes the address and travels north. He doesn't want to draw attention to the van driving through the area. He calls Hatfield after returning to Contys Motel.

"John. What kind of license tag was on the car found near the escape route?"

"I will find out for you. Hold on." A moment later he returns and says, "It was a Florida temporary tag. You got something?"

"I want you to look up information on the following address and let me know what you find out."

After receiving the information John says, "I'll be in touch."

Peter showered and tried to relax but the anticipation was too high. He scours google maps satellite view to get a bird's eye and street view of the trailer. Seeing the water around the property, he travels into town to reconnoiter. It did not take long to find what he was looking for next to a house on the edge of town. There were small 12-foot kayaks. They were bright orange, yellow, and a dark green one. He did not want to buy one and have it traced back to him, so he went down the street with the rod and reels and put on one of the Skinny Matters fishing shirts and hats. He stood on the side of the road at a bridge to the south of the Observatory tower fishing. He watched all

146

the traffic on the road and boat traffic moving into the bay. His phone rang and he saw it was John.

"Go ahead."

"That address is a local family owner, but it is currently rented."

"Thanks. I'll let you know if I come up with more."

# 49

There was not a lot of traffic on the road in the stifling and humid heat of summer. Peter took out a rod and reel. He notices it had a Mirrolure tied to the end of a two-foot piece of leader. The General had the right saltwater combination, he thought to himself. With the sun high, the water was heated, and most fish will be in deeper water or under the shade of the mangroves. Peter looks up as a Chevrolet Suburban passes him traveling southbound. With the dark tinted windows there was no way to see inside but it was not his target vehicle. He sees the SUV pass northbound and other cars pass back and forth. No Toyota Corolla's.

He waits until almost dark and eats and drinks from a cooler he had packed near Naples. He drives over near the house with the kayaks as the sun sets.

"Still no lights." He says to himself.

Returning to Contys hotel, he rinses in a cold shower, no soap to lessen odors. Toweling off, Peter calls Rafi.

Rafi answers on the first few rings before Peter has the chance to respond ask, "Peter where the hell are you?"

"Working a few leads and running a couple of errands for John."

"Like what?"

"Logistical issues. What about you and that end?" Peter asked to get Rafi off questioning him.

"Remember the extra bodies on the shrimp boat?"

"Yeah."

"They are the missing crew members from the shrimp docks. Don't know why they were there. The thought is they snooped and got caught and the boat captain, now identified as Pedro Gomez, didn't want the police around."

"Makes sense. What do you know about Gomez?"

"Mexican national. Ties with cartels. The Gulf Cartel specifically. Looks like he stole the boat he was Captain of in Corpus Christi, Texas. Left with a first mate and the boat owner a month ago and never heard from again. It was assumed they were lost at sea. Coast Guard search ended after a few days. Showed up here and operating from the guest dock at the Tampa Shrimp Docks on Causeway."

"What about the others at the house and other boats?"

"Working on them but they appear to be Venezuelan and middle eastern."

"Interesting. You know who is connected to Venezuela?"

"Venezuelans? Sure, the Iranian connections are strong." Rafi responded.

"Okay. Keep me up to date. Talk with you later." Peter hung up the phone before Rafi could ask him anything.

Rafi looked over at a couple of the tech guys. "I need you to look something else up for me. Get the location of this phone. Make it a priority."

He gave them Peter's phone number.

Peter laid down while hydrating with water. At 10:00 PM he got dressed in dark BDU's and grabbed the mosquito jacket. He picked up his go-bag and went to the van. Driving past the kayak house there is still no signs of people. Parking down the street he walks back to the rear of the house and moves to the side with the kayaks.

Talking to himself saying, "I have got to be careful. Cannot imagine getting caught committing a felony theft right now."

He moves with caution to the green camo kayak. The two-sided paddle is bungeed to the inside of the craft. It's light so he walks it back to his van and slides it inside. He had removed the dome lights to prevent illumination of the interior.

He drives down the street to the bridge that allows boats to pass into the Ten-Thousand Islands from Lake Placid. Lake Placid is the head of the canal that runs along the east side of the city. After a few minutes, he doesn't see anyone and walks back to the van, removes the kayak, lays his go-bag inside and walks it under the bridge. He takes one last look around and slides the plastic craft into the water, climbs inside and paddles south.

It's past 11:00 PM and Peter has a mile to paddle. Attaching a night vision scope, he looks around the area. He can hear occasional movements along the banks and in the waters and knows they are the sounds of alligators. They are everywhere and he does not want to fall out of the kayak. Ahead he sees lights of the houses and he paddles with caution not to make noise. By midnight he approaches a small dirt road he saw earlier in the day. Pulling to the edge he climbs out of the kayak and for a moment feels exposed as he must stand in ankle deep water. He would be easy prey for an alligator who followed his movements, ease up on him, grab him by the leg and begin the death spin. Alligators spin when they grab prey to help subdue before taking the meal underwater and lodging it under a log to feed later. The spin itself will break his leg preventing an escape. Peter knows he cannot turn on his light. Anyone looking in the direction would see and investigate at this time of the morning.

Making it to hard ground Peter waste no time in pulling the kayak out of the water and into the weeds. He removes what he needs from the bag and places it in the weeds near the kayak and moves towards the trailer a block away. Easing up to a lifted trailer that appeared abandoned he got underneath and stopped. On the side of the trailer, he sees a dark colored Suburban with dark window tint.

Thinking to himself, "It's the same one I saw earlier today. Just my luck the owners arrived home on the same night I wanted to use the trailer to scope out the target."

Peter sat quiet listening for any sounds from the trailer floor above indicating the occupants are awake. Hearing none he moves forward. The lights are on at the targeted trailer in the back and he steps closer to the opposite side. Approaching and smelling cigarette smoke, he stops. He steps toward the front and sees a man on the step smoking. He is dressed more like a lookout rather than a resident stepping outside this early in the morning for a smoke. "That's odd. How many people are in there?" he thinks to himself.

Moving down to the other end of the trailer he hears men talking. Several sound angry and they are speaking not Spanish as thought, but it sounds…middle eastern. Republican Guard members getting the third world Venezuelans to do some of their heavy lifting. He moves to the front again and sees the guard standing with an AK47 over his shoulder. The weapon is not on the ready so he is there to watch but not expecting anyone. These are either our guys or South American drug cartel members. Either way, they don't belong. They chose their path of destruction. Terrorism and drug cartels are all related. Money made for financial support and killers to ensure the financial support.

Peter pulls his KBar and moves to the left of the steps. He picks up a stick and tosses it to the other side. The guard stops smoking and looks to his right. He still expects nothing, not removing the slung rifle. He moves down the steps and stops before the bottom and turns on a flashlight to look for the source of the sounds.

Good for Peter because the light will cause him to lose his night vision and he steps up behind him, wraps his left hand over the man's mouth, and pulls him hard over the railing and down to the ground. With the base of the knife, he strikes him in the back of the head. Peter thinks he doesn't want to kill him in case he wasn't who he thought. Zip tied hands and feet, duct tape over his mouth, Peter moves up the steps. At the door he listens and checks the handle. As expected, it's open because of the guard outside. Easing it open Peter steps into the living room with his Glock in hand. He sweeps the room and moves to the left and into the hallway towards the voices in the rear of the trailer.

"Drop the gun! A voice sounds behind him.

# 50

Peter laid the gun down allowing him the opportunity to slide the KBar up his sleeve.

"Come in and join us." A woman's voice says as Zarrin Banu walks around the corner.

"Who are you?"

"A neighbor. Saw all the activity and was making sure the place wasn't broken in to."

"Check him for weapons and secure him." She said to the man behind him.

The man stepped forward and patted him down. Cursory pat down, not a complete search. He removed the revolver and the Emerson knife but did not touch his arms. Using zip ties, he secured his hands.

"Come in. What is your name?"

"Peter, what is yours?"

"I saw you fishing earlier on the side of the road."

"I was. Is that what you're doing? Looking for fishing locations?"

He did not want to say that he had seen their vehicle earlier. The implication is that he notices too much.

"And the night vision?"

"I like to fish at night. Gotta be able to see. Look, why are you asking me these questions. Why am I tied up? You're the one who should be concerned. The cops are on their way. I called them when I saw all the activity. Leave now and I never saw anybody."

"No, Peter. Not yet. Had you called the police you would have waited to watch when they arrived. Who do you work for?"

"Where is Garshasps?" She asked the others.

Another man moved passed her towards the front of the trailer to look for the man Peter tied up. Middle eastern for sure Peter thought to himself.

"Self-employed fishing guide. Like I said, if you want to go fishing."

"Shut up!" She raised her voice.

"Bring him into the bathroom."

Pushed along, Peter walks through the master bedroom and glances around. As he enters the bathroom, he is set back by what he sees. Two men cut up in the bathtub. At least he could see two heads. There were arms, intestines, and other body parts. They were putting them in large garbage bags and then into coolers. They did not count on being disturbed.

"Whoa there a moment! What the hell! I have not seen anything! Let me go and as far as I'm concerned nothing happened. This is after all the Everglades." Peter said with concern.

"We are, how do you say, removing loose ends." Zarrin responded.

The man who stepped outside returned and spoke to her, but Peter could not understand the words but knew what he was saying.

"See. I did not hurt your guy. I'm just a fishing guide." Peter said trying to take advantage of the moment noticing that only the guy who had tied him up and another were behind him.

Peter dropped to his knees and started pleading. The distraction allowed him to slide the knife into his hand and under the zip tie. Feeling it break under the struggle and fainting a fear reaction, the man behind him reaches down to grab him. He has positioned the knife with the cutting blade forward, an action created from tactical training. As the man brought him up, Peter waits until he felt his balance and with one punch, forces the blade across the man's neck and drives it down again between his clavicle and neck. A certain death blow as the man's subclavian artery severs in his upper chest and blood blows onto the ceiling. This causes enough surprise and pause to the others allowing Peter to remove his Glock from the falling man's waistband and fire a single round into the chest of the other man. Running for the front door, Peter knows the other man, the sentry, is waiting outside. He opens the door and sprints down the stairs. The man had recovered from his concussion enough to try and focus on who was coming through the door. This was enough time for Peter to strike him and knock him over the side railings. Another man was coming through the door behind him. To retrace the areas he was familiar, he ran towards the dirt road and the place where his go-bag was waiting with the kayak. He had an M4 with extra magazines and that would give him the firepower he needs. He reaches the location, but his eyes were still trying to adjust to the dark. Tripping over the kayak he can hear the other man running behind him and closing fast. He feels the bag and tries to open it when he is hit from the side and driven towards the water, falling face down. Peter tries to stand yet the man was still on his feet and holding him down. The muddy bottom preventing Peter from getting traction to stand and the man held him pinned face down underwater. Without traction he was unable to recover and felt his consciousness fading.

Another weight hit him and for a fleeting second Peter knew this is over. He will not be able to fight off two of them. From underwater he hears screams and another weight steps on him. It's different and heavier. At that moment, the man flips off him and he and the other start spinning in the water. Peter gets his head above water, grasping for air and out of instinct and adrenaline crawls for shore. Being held in the water and on the bottom, the ancient predator was attracted to the sounds of the men in the water and attacked where all his meals begin, above the surface. Making it to shore he can still hear the thrashing in the water, and it intensifies as other alligators arrive trying to indulge in the fresh kill.

The woman and at least the other sentry are still at the trailer. He gets to his bag and removes the rifle and again approaches the trailer. The Suburban is gone. He doesn't see the sentry by the door and makes entry. Moving with the rifle short stocked down the hall he tries his best to clear the rooms and closets. In the master bedroom he sees the blood pool from the man he killed and the cut-up bodies in the tub, but no one else. They had removed their men and fled in the SUV. He steps outside as another SUV pulls up followed by several police cars.

# 51

Several armed men exit the vehicle and the right front passenger yells out, "Peter. Are you ok? Do you need an ambulance?"

It was Rafi and other team members. The police units surrounded the trailer and make entry. Seeing what was inside, the scene is secured.

"Rafi. How the hell did you...? And then he stopped. "You tracked my phone when I called you."

"Yes, I did. You didn't tell me, and I had to know where to get to you. Then as we are coming into town, we find out that the police were getting calls about shots and screams from here."

"We need a BOLO on a dark colored Suburban. There will be a dead man, maybe a second, and a woman and an injured man inside. Tell them they are armed and dangerous."

The police officer standing nearby placed the announcement on his hand-held radio. He looks up and says, "I put it out but everyone in the area is here. I'll expand it to the State Troopers and the City of Naples as well."

"Rafi." Peter said.

"Get on your phone and start spreading the word to all our contacts. I think the remaining members of the assault group on MacDill are inside in the master bathroom. Can I borrow another phone? I need to call John."

Peter stepped away and made the call. John answered on the second ring.

"Hello?"

"John. Peter. Had to borrow another phone. I got to them but someone else beat me to it."

"Ok. Tell me when we are secure."

"Roger that." Peter hung up the phone.

More police arrive and John sent other assets to the area so Peter could leave. From Contys Peter called him back.

"Peter, go to the airport in Naples. I have a jet landing in 30 minutes. Take it back to Miami. I will take care of all your stuff."

Arriving in Miami another SUV met up with Peter. Driving him towards Bal Harbor in North Miami Beach, they arrived at a gated home. The gates opened and Peter went inside.

"Dinner? You hungry?" John asked.

"Hadn't thought about it but yes I am."

"Steak how?

"Medium rare."

John picked up the phone and pushed a button. "Two Ribeye's. Medium rare." And hung up.

Sitting on the couch, John poured them each tall Bourbons and started to explain.

"We have some preliminary information. The guys in the tub and coolers were Venezuelan. They have been identified as Jose Arriba and the other, he paused, Tomas Fauzi Guerra. They are our guys and the one who murdered the Border Patrol agents. Locals are going to call this a drug murder. Someone watched the murder scene in *Scarface* too many times. Rafi and the others found the kayak and will see that it is returned. Local boys playing games must have stolen it. As far as the one in the water, nothing found. Big alligators in there though. Don't think we'll push that issue. As for the others who got away, we are working with our foreign counterparts to get identifications. I will call on you from time to time and have you look at pictures. We gave them the name you heard but it is a common Persian first name. They removed everything that could get traced back to Iran. We know the hit was orchestrated by them. We will respond in time. We want to know by who. They are not sure if we caught the one that tried to kill you in the water or if we captured him and must look over their shoulder. The irony is they intended to do the same thing to the Venezuelans. No other reason to move those body parts to coolers but feed them to the gators."

"What now?" Peter asked.

"Everyone is impressed, and heads are rolling for not providing the necessary help when asked. Things are changing Peter. I want you to lead that change. We have the backing from the top office and unlimited funding."

He hesitated a moment, looked up at Peter and said, "Are you in?"

"Can I shower before dinner?"

"Sure. I'm sorry. Down the hall there on the right. You'll find everything you need in the bathroom pantry."

"Thanks."

Peter walks toward the bathroom and turns looking at John, finishing his bourbon and said, "Yes."

About the Author

Steven Varnell is a retired State Trooper and law enforcement certified instructor. He has taught police topics to his own and numerous other city, county, state, and federal agencies. Steve is a certified Interviews and Interrogations and High Liability instructor. As an adjunct instructor for St Petersburg College and his own company, Interviewing and Survival Strategies, he taught police agencies throughout the country at every level, courses in interdiction, officer safety, patrol, interviews, interrogations, behavior analysis, and written statement analysis.

Steve has received recognition by nearly every federal, local, county, and state law enforcement agencies. He is the only law enforcement officer to receive the Officer of the Year award in Hillsborough County, Florida three separate times for his work in drug investigations. He received a commendation award by the International Narcotic Officers Association, presented at Reno, Nevada in 1993. He is also the recipient of the annual ASIS International Law Enforcement Recognition Award (2006) for his work in narcotics investigations.